M.C. B  **gely** successful
Aga ha Ra h and Edwardian

DUNS

b
Cou

book is due for return on or before the last da

£2-20

Titles by M.C. Beaton

The Travelling Matchmaker series

Emily Goes to Exeter • *Belinda Goes to Bath*
Penelope Goes to Portsmouth • *Beatrice Goes to Brighton*
Deborah Goes to Dover • *Yvonne Goes to York*

The Edwardian Murder Mystery series

Snobbery with Violence • *Hasty Death*
Sick of Shadows • *Our Lady of Pain*

The Agatha Raisin series

Agatha Raisin and the Quiche of Death • *Agatha Raisin and the Vicious Vet*
Agatha Raisin and the Potted Gardener • *Agatha Raisin and the Walkers of Dembley*
Agatha Raisin and the Murderous Marriage
Agatha Raisin and the Terrible Tourist
Agatha Raisin and the Wellspring of Death
Agatha Raisin and the Wizard of Evesham
Agatha Raisin and the Witch of Wyckhadden
Agatha Raisin and the Fairies of Fryfam
Agatha Raisin and the Love from Hell
Agatha Raisin and the Day the Floods Came
Agatha Raisin and the Curious Curate • *Agatha Raisin and the Haunted House*
Agatha Raisin and the Deadly Dance • *Agatha Raisin and the Perfect Paragon*
Agatha Raisin and Love, Lies and Liquor
Agatha Raisin and Kissing Christmas Goodbye
Agatha Raisin and a Spoonful of Poison • *Agatha Raisin: There Goes the Bride*
Agatha Raisin and the Busy Body

The Hamish Macbeth series

Death of a Gossip • *Death of a Cad*
Death of an Outsider • *Death of a Perfect Wife*
Death of a Hussy • *Death of a Snob*
Death of a Prankster • *Death of a Glutton*
Death of a Travelling Man • *Death of a Charming Man*
Death of a Nag • *Death of a Macho Man*
Death of a Dentist • *Death of a Scriptwriter*
Death of an Addict • *A Highland Christmas*
Death of a Dustman • *Death of a Celebrity*
Death of a Village • *Death of a Poison Pen*
Death of a Bore • *Death of a Dreamer*
Death of a Maid • *Death of a Gentle Lady*
Death of a Witch • *Death of a Valentine*
Death of a Sweep

Belinda Goes To Bath

Being the Second Volume of the
Travelling Matchmaker

M. C. BEATON

ROBINSON

Constable & Robinson Ltd
3 The Lanchesters
162 Fulham Palace Road
London W6 9ER
www.constablerobinson.com

First published in the US by St Martin's Press, 1991

First published in the UK by Robinson,
an imprint of Constable & Robinson Ltd, 2011

A copy of the British Library Cataloguing in
Publication data is available from the British Library

ISBN: 978-1-84901-480-9

Typeset by TW Typesetting, Plymouth, Devon

Printed and bound in the EU

3 5 7 9 10 8 6 4

1

Wickedness is a myth invented by good people to account for the curious attractiveness of others.

Oscar Wilde

Hannah Pym arose at four in the morning in a bedroom in the Bell Savage Inn in the City of London and prepared for adventure.

For Hannah, adventure lay in the Flying Machines, as the stage-coaches were called. A legacy left her by a late employer had given her new freedom. She had already made one journey to Exeter and had had many adventures, which had only whetted her appetite for more.

She lived in Kensington, and the thickening fog of the day before had made her take the precaution of travelling to London and booking a room for the night at the inn so as to be in time for the coach in the morning. She lit a tallow candle on the mantelpiece of her bedchamber and carried it to the toilet table, where she sat down and studied her face in the glass.

Hannah had taken to studying herself closely in the glass since her last journey, not because she thought she was beautiful, for she knew she was not, but to see if she had begun to look like a lady. Her late employer's brother, Sir George Clarence, had befriended Hannah Pym, ex-housekeeper now and, thanks to his brother's generous legacy, a lady of independent means. Hannah was flattered and pleased at this new and unlikely friendship and hoped that the elevation to such distinguished company would begin to show in her features.

Her gown was of fine cambric and her linen of the best because of Sir George's suggestion that she help herself to Mrs Clarence's wardrobe. Mrs Clarence was the wife of Hannah's late employer, who had run off years ago with a footman, leaving her clothes behind. The clothes were all very well, thought Hannah, but it was the face that was the problem. She was middle-aged, in her forties, with thick sandy hair and large, odd eyes that seemed to change colour according to her mood. Her nose was slightly crooked, her skin sallow, and her mouth long and humorous. Her figure was distressingly thin and flat-chested, but she had fine hands and neat ankles and long, slender feet. It was the eyes that betrayed her late servant status, thought Hannah. Ladies had hard, autocratic stares. They did not have curious, eager eyes.

Hannah felt she could not expect such adventures as she had experienced on her last journey on the Exeter road, when she and her fellow passengers had been drawn together by accident, robbery and snowstorm. Hannah knew that it was possible for a coachful of people to travel long distances without saying a single word, English reserve always triumphing over curiosity.

From down below came the bustle of preparation. The coach she was to take to Bath – no, *The* Bath, Hannah corrected herself; only people who did not know the glories of travel referred to that city as just 'Bath' – was called The Quicksilver. She wondered what her fellow passengers would be like and then reminded herself sadly that it did not befit her new station in life to be nosy about other people. She practised haughty indifference in the glass, but decided she looked silly and pulled her nose in distress.

She rose from the toilet table and packed her trunk. Then, with a feeling of great daring, she put on her head a velvet turban with a 'banditti' plume and a veil hanging to the shoulders.

Hannah had paid her shot in advance. The inn waiters were hovering in the corridors, eager hands outstretched for tips. Hannah parted with some small change and then went out into the foggy courtyard. She gave her ticket to the coachman, noting that he was a dandified young man in a double-breasted coat and with a wide, low-crowned hat. Most coachmen were like Old Tom of her previous journey, fat and

3

grog-faced and muffled in shawls. But this coachman belonged to the new, younger breed. He had adopted a haughty, supercilious air and looked as if he was hoping for the arrival of some outsiders to talk down to. The outsiders were the people who paid half-fare to travel on the roof of the coach. But it seemed that Hannah was the first arrival.

She stood for a moment surveying the coach. It was a new, smart turnout with high red wheels but with the body of the coach covered in the usual studded black leather, the oval windows being picked out in red. She climbed inside.

The early morning was freezing cold, and she could smell the fog, a sulphurous smell that seemed to emanate from the hell it created to the London onlooker's eye. Figures outside the coach flitted in its gloom like demons. Who would the other passengers be? thought Hannah. An article in a magazine she'd read said the passengers of coaches usually consisted of one drunken sailor, one lawyer, one military gentleman, one mother with a nauseous child, and one faded lady who always complained mendaciously that her own private coach had gone ahead with her baggage.

The coach door opened on the far side from where Hannah sat and a couple climbed in. Hannah flicked a curious glance at them. The woman was small and pretty in a kittenish way and the man was handsome in a regular, uninteresting fashion. He helped her to a corner seat before taking the seat opposite and she thanked him effusively, calling him Mr Judd, and he

4

replied, calling her Mrs Judd. A dull married couple, guessed Hannah, hoping the other passengers might prove to be more entertaining.

There was a rattle of wheels in the courtyard and Hannah rubbed at the glass with her glove and looked out to see an expensive carriage rolling into the courtyard. A coachman in splendid livery of scarlet and gold sat on the box and two footmen stood on the backstrap. The carriage drew up alongside the coach. The footmen jumped down and opened the carriage door and let down the steps. A young lady, fashionably dressed, got down, followed by a stern, middle-aged woman. The footmen then started to unload a quantity of luggage from the roof and hand it up to the guard of the coach.

The dandified coachman opened the door of the coach and ushered both ladies in, bowing very low. The young lady took a seat in the corner opposite Hannah and her companion sat beside her.

Hannah immediately noticed that the girl had been crying. Not that her eyes were puffy and red, but there was a weary sadness about them.

The girl saw Hannah looking at her and gave a tentative smile; her companion frowned awfully and tapped the girl on the wrist in an admonitory way before throwing Hannah a haughty look.

The coach dipped and swayed as the coachman climbed up on to his box. The guard sent out a triumphant fanfare and The Quicksilver set out slowly on its way into the blinding, choking fog.

The roads would be frozen hard, thought Hannah,

so there was no danger of their being stuck in the mud outside the village of Knightsbridge. Her eyes began to feel sore with the strain of peering out as she searched for familiar landmarks. Inside the coach was an ivory timetable lit by an oil-lamp, marking out the times and stages of their route.

The soft light of the lamp fell on the girl's face. She had fallen asleep, as had her companion, so Hannah had an opportunity to study them both at leisure. The girl was not beautiful. She had a thin, sensitive face and high cheek-bones, which were considered most unfashionable in an age when women wore wax pads inside their cheeks to give them the required Dutch-doll effect. Her mouth was full and sensitive and peculiarly sensual, and the lashes that covered her eyes were long and silky. Under her bonnet, her slate-coloured hair was fine and wispy.

Her companion was rigidly corseted. She had the bosom and profile of a figurehead on a ship. Her clothes were fine but looked as if they had been made for someone else. The servant part of Hannah's mind decided they probably had been. This woman was a paid companion and the clothes had probably belonged at one time to an employer.

Hannah turned her attention back to the outside world. The fog was thick. They would soon be nearing Kensington and Thornton Hall, where she had lived all those long years, working her way up from scullery maid to the rank of housekeeper. Sir George Clarence, who had inherited the Hall, had told her that he had started work on the gardens. Hannah had looked forward to seeing the improvements, but the fog blanketed everything.

She tugged at the strap and let down the window and hung out. The Quicksilver was travelling in a line of coaches and mail coaches, one lighting the way for the other. She could see their torches flaring up ahead, but as for the scenery at the side of the road, she could not even make out where she was.

She sank back in her seat with a little sigh and jerked up the glass.

She found the other passengers awake and looking at her with varying degrees of outrage. 'Have you no consideration for others?' demanded Mr Judd. 'My wife is most delicate. Are you not delicate, my dear?'

'Yes, Mr Judd,' said his wife in a low voice.

Then the young lady's companion gave tongue. 'I have a delicate chest,' she said, tapping that huge part of her body. 'Do not dare to open that window again.'

'I am sorry,' said Hannah mildly. 'I wondered where we were. A friend of mine has a house outside the village of Kensington and he told me he was working on the gardens and I was anxious to see the improvements.'

'And could you see anything?' asked the girl. Her eyes appeared to be a sort of greenish-grey, Hannah noticed.

Hannah shook her head. 'The fog is very thick,' she said. 'We are travelling slowly in a convoy with other coaches and mail coaches.'

'We shall never reach The Bath at this rate,' said Mr Judd crossly.

Hannah thought the young lady opposite muttered, 'Good,' but could not be sure.

After they seemed to have been travelling for a considerable time, the coach stopped. Hannah looked out again. 'Why, we have only reached The Half-Way House at Knightsbridge,' she exclaimed.

'Disgraceful!' said Mr Judd. 'Is it not?'

He glared at his wife, who had been half asleep. She promptly sat up straight and said, 'Yes, dear,' in a mechanical voice.

The coach door opened to reveal a waiter with a tray. He handed round tankards containing a steaming-hot mixture of milk and rum and nutmeg.

'What is in this?' demanded the companion suspiciously.

Hannah realized the young lady was looking at her with a sort of appeal in those strange eyes of hers. 'It is an innocuous beverage,' said Hannah.

By the time the companion had sipped hers and discovered there was a large measure of rum in it, the young lady had finished hers off.

At last the coach moved off again, crawling over the cobblestones of Knightsbridge. The cold was intense. Hannah, although she was wrapped in a fur-lined cloak and was wearing two flannel petticoats under her dress, began to feel quite sick.

She buried her feet in the straw on the floor, seeking warmth and finding none.

'I am so very cold,' said Mrs Judd suddenly.

'We are all very cold,' said her husband repressively. 'Contain yourself.'

She is going to say, 'Yes, dear,' thought Hannah, and Mrs Judd did.

It was all very well for her husband, thought Hannah crossly. He was enveloped in a greatcoat over a coat and breeches and two waistcoats. His wife's cloak was not very thick and under it she was wearing a sky-blue muslin gown.

Because of the thinness of fashionable gowns, it was estimated that at least eighteen thousand women dropped dead of cold during the English winters. When Hannah had read that figure in the newspaper she had thought it a wild exaggeration, but now she was not so sure. Women had even abandoned their stays. It was almost a point of honour to appear in all seasons in the most delicate of muslins.

The girl opposite Hannah suddenly leaned forward and held out a gloved hand. 'I am Miss Belinda Earle,' she said, 'and this is my companion, Miss Wimple.'

Miss Wimple bridled. 'Really, Miss Earle. Such familiarity.'

'And I,' said Hannah pleasantly and firmly, 'am Miss Hannah Pym and very pleased to make your aquaintance.'

Miss Wimple tapped Belinda again on the wrist as a warning against further intimacies, but Belinda, whose spirits seemed to be recovering despite the cold, ignored her.

'And why do you journey to The Bath?' she asked Hannah.

'I am travelling because I like travelling,' said Hannah. 'I have never been to The Bath and wished to see it.'

'In a freezing fog? In mid-winter?' Belinda sounded half-incredulous, half-amused.

Hannah gave a reluctant laugh. 'I am ever optimistic, Miss Earle. I am sure the sun will rise and we shall find ourselves out of the fog. At least in this procession of coaches, we shall be safe from highwaymen on Hounslow Heath, unless the ghost of the Duke of Richmond's page appears to haunt us.'

'Who was he?' asked Belinda. She shrugged off her companion's hand crossly. 'Miss Wimple, if we are to pass this freezing cold, uncomfortable journey, it would help to be amused. Tell me about the Duke of Richmond's page, Miss Pym.'

Hannah settled back in her seat. She had read a great number of books about the highways of England and the adventures that had taken place on them.

'His name was Claude Duval,' said Hannah, 'and he was the greatest of highwaymen. He was born at Domfront in Normandy. His father was a miller and his mother a tailor's daughter. He travelled to Paris and did odd jobs for Englishmen and eventually made his way to England in time for the Restoration, where he entered the service of the Duke of Richmond. He was a gifted and elegant ruffian. He gamed and drank and soon took to villainy to help pay his debts. He was finally arrested at the Hole in the Wall in Chandos Street, committed to Newgate, arraigned, convicted, and condemned, and on Friday, January twenty-first, 1670, executed at Tyburn. He was only twenty-seven years old. It was said he was a man after Charles the Second's heart and not unlike him, except that he was better looking. It was also said that the king would have spared Duval if he had had his way.

'Duval was buried in the middle aisle of Covent Garden Church. The ladies made up the largest part of the crowd in attendance. Flambeaus blazed and the hero was laid under a white marble stone on which you can still read this inscription:

DU VALL'S EPITAPH

Here lies Du Vall: Reader If Male thou art
Look to thy Purse: if Female to thy Heart.
Much Havoc has he made of both; for all
Men he made stand and Women he made fall.
The second Conqu'ror of the Norman Race
Knights to his arms did yield and Ladies to his
    Face.
Old Tyburn's glory, England's illustrious Thief,
Du Vall the Ladies' joy; Du Vall the Ladies Grief.

'His name was spelled D-u-v-a-l, in one word, but on the tomb it is Anglicized and spelled 'D-u V-a-l-l, two words. 'Twas said that ladies travelled over Hounslow Heath praying he might stop their coaches.'

'How romantic,' sighed Mrs Judd.

'Fiddlesticks,' said her husband. 'A thief romantic? Of what can you be thinking, Mrs Judd?'

'My apologies, my love,' said his wife faintly. 'It is the intense cold, you see.'

'Do not utter such foolishness again,' he snapped.

The coach lurched and began to roll forward, gaining speed. Hannah looked out of the window.

They were clear of the fog and the sky was turning light grey. But they were now past Kensington and she would have no opportunity of catching a glimpse of Thornton Hall or of its gardens.

'We shall breakfast soon,' she said cheerfully. And after a few miles, the coach rolled into an inn yard and the stiff and frozen passengers climbed down.

Hannah thought in that moment that there ought to be a hymn of praise to the English coaching inn. Blazing fires greeted them, and the air was redolent with the smells of hot coffee, fresh bread and bacon.

Before she could sit down at the table, Miss Wimple drew Hannah aside. 'Do not encourage my charge to prattle. She must be kept aware at all times that she is being sent away to The Bath in disgrace.'

'Why? What did she do?' asked Hannah, her odd eyes snapping with curiosity.

'My lips are sealed,' said Miss Wimple.

As soon as breakfast was over, Hannah slipped away and asked the landlord if the ladies of the party might have the use of a bedchamber in which to put on some more warm clothes, and also if hot bricks could be put on the carriage floor. She tipped the landlord generously and then had to tip the coachman equally generously so that the ladies' trunks might be unloaded.

Mr Judd said firmly that his wife was very well as she was. Hannah ignored him and addressed Mrs Judd directly. 'I have a spare cloak in my trunk. If you put it over your own, you would be so much warmer.'

She cast a scared, rabbit-like look at her husband.

'Come along with me,' said Hannah bracingly. 'We shall only be a moment, Mr Judd.'

She led Mrs Judd up the stairs and Belinda and Miss Wimple followed.

'This is an excellent idea,' said Belinda, throwing back the lid of a trunk. 'I am going to put on two more petticoats.' Even Miss Wimple seemed to be thawing towards Hannah as she took a large shawl out of her own baggage and wrapped it around her massive shoulders.

Hannah found a scarlet merino cloak and insisted Mrs Judd put it on over her own.

It was a much more cheerful party that set out on the road again, all exclaiming with gratitude at the heat provided by hot bricks placed in the straw on the carriage floor. Mr Judd did slightly sour the atmosphere by lecturing his wife on having borrowed Hannah's cloak, but Hannah noticed that Mrs Judd drew the scarlet cloak more tightly about her and that her soft mouth was folded into a firm line of defiance.

A red sun rose, sparkling on frost-covered fields. Bare branches of trees stood out skeletal and black against the red sky.

Mrs Judd fell asleep first, followed by her husband and then Miss Wimple.

'Heigh-ho,' said Belinda to Hannah, 'we are travelling at some speed now.'

'You arrived at the Bell Savage in an extremely handsome carriage,' said Hannah. 'I am surprised you took the stage.'

'I am in disgrace, you see,' said Belinda calmly. 'My uncle and aunt said they had already spent a fortune

13

on trying to marry me off and were not going to waste any money on me. I am being sent to my Great-Aunt Harriet in The Bath. She is a very religious old lady and is to teach me the folly or my ways.'

'That folly being . . . ?'

Belinda glanced at the sleeping occupants of the carriage and then leaned forward. 'I ran away with a footman,' she said.

Hannah looked at her sympathetically. Mrs Clarence, wife of her late employer, had done just that; pretty, witty, gay Mrs Clarence, whose going had sent Thornton Hall into a sort of perpetual mourning.

'Tell me about it,' said Hannah.

'Are you not shocked?'

Hannah shook her head.

'I had better tell you how it all came about.' Belinda gave a little sigh. 'I am nineteen years of age. Mama and Papa died of the smallpox two years ago. I inherit all their money when I am twenty-one or when I become married. Papa was a scholarly man and Mama was very pretty, not like me. My uncle and aunt, Mr and Mrs Earle – my uncle is my father's brother – are quite different. They are very rigid and very high in the instep. My fortune impressed them with the idea that it would be simple to find a duke or an earl for me to marry. To that end, they brought me out at the last Season and then again at the Little Season. I did not take. Or rather, there were actually several gentlemen interested in me but they were not titled and so were discouraged. My aunt and uncle said there was a certain lack of necessary innocence

14

in my appearance which attracted the wrong type of gentlemen. I tried to explain to them that when I reached the age of twenty-one, I would be independently wealthy and could travel and study and would not have to marry at all. They were shocked. They said it had been my dead mother's dearest wish that I marry, and so they said that I must endure another Season this year.

'It is so very lowering,' said Belinda, 'to have to sit at balls, propping up the wall. Of course, I attracted adventurers from time to time and, for some reason, elderly roués.'

Looking at that oddly passionate mouth, Hannah thought she knew why.

'As I explained, my uncle and aunt felt I lacked the dewy innocence of appearance necessary in a debutante and hired Miss Wimple to school me in the arts of flirtation.'

'How can a middle-aged spinster be expected to school a young lady in the arts of flirtation?' asked Hannah.

'Middle-aged ladies are supposed to know everything. Oh, I beg your pardon.' Belinda coloured.

Hannah laughed. 'Never mind my sensibilities. Go on with your story.'

'In our household, there was this footman. His name was Patrick Sullivan.'

'Irish,' said Hannah sympathetically.

'Yes, Irish, and with all the charm of that race. He had thick black curls . . .'

Hannah raised her eyebrows, momentarily shocked.

'I saw him out of powder once when he was returning from a funeral,' explained Belinda. 'He always seemed to be asking leave to go to funerals. It was found out afterwards that he did not have one relative in this country, but liked to invent funerals so as to get free time. He had very merry blue eyes. He was most disrespectful behind Aunt and Uncle's backs,' said Belinda with a giggle. 'He called them the Cod and Codess, and they are rather cold and fishlike, with pale eyes and thick lips.

'I told Patrick I was becoming desperate at the idea of another Season and he startled me by saying, "Run away with me." I must have been mad, and it all seems so very shocking now. But I thought he wanted to marry me. You see, with my money, he would be rich and he was so merry and bright, I thought we would have a glorious time.

'I did not climb out of the window or anything like that. Patrick had it all arranged. He waited until my uncle and aunt were out walking, I packed a bag, and we simply walked from the house and took a hack to the City.

'But when we got to the City, he tipped his hat to me and said he hoped I would be happy now that I was free, and started to walk away. I ran after him and said, "But we are to be married, Patrick."

'He said he had no intention of marrying me but was going on to a new position in Lord Cunningham's household in Grosvenor Square. I said he had no need to work any more. As soon as we were married I would get my fortune. But Patrick had read the terms

16

of my parents' will in my uncle's desk, which I had not. I was to have my fortune if I married before the age of twenty-one, but I had to marry someone of whom *my uncle and aunt approved.* "But where am I to go?" I asked him. He scratched his head and said, faith, I'd surely scores of relatives that were more congenial, and when I told him I had not, he said I had better go home before I was missed.

'I shall always remember him walking away from me . . . clank, clank, clank.'

Hannah looked puzzled. 'Clank, clank . . . ? Oh, you are speaking metaphorically. Do you mean like a knight in shining armour?'

Belinda shook her head. 'No, nothing like that. It was the spoons, do you see? He had stolen the silver.'

Hannah tried to keep a straight face but she began to laugh and Belinda started to laugh as well.

'So,' said Hannah at last, mopping her streaming eyes, 'I suppose you must survive until twenty-one?'

'So long away,' said Belinda mournfully, and Hannah had a sudden sharp memory of youth, when the years had been very long. Now they seemed to speed by.

'There is always the possibility of romance,' said Hannah.

'Pooh. How much better to be free and single.' Belinda lowered her voice and glanced at the sleeping Judds. 'Now there is a typical marriage.'

Hannah frowned. She herself thought the Judds's marriage was indeed typical but she was not going to agree with Belinda. Young women should all get married and have children. That was Hannah's firm belief. It was different for someone like herself. Ambitious servants knew they could not marry.

'You might meet someone in Bath.' Hannah had become tired of saying 'The' Bath. It sounded vaguely indecent anyway.

'I shall never meet anyone,' said Belinda firmly.

'But think, my dear, although you may not have attracted certain titled gentlemen, was there no one you met during the Season who attracted you in the least?'

'Not one.'

'In any case, since you are here, I assume when you arrived home that day your disappearance had been noticed?'

'Oh, yes. And oh, the folly of it. I had left a note, you see, telling them that I must have my freedom. And so it was decided to reform me.' Belinda sighed. 'Travel on the stage does seem a sort of purgatory.'

'Is your great-aunt so very strict?'

'Yes, she has turned Methodist, you see. I shall simply have to be patient until I am twenty-one.'

'And then what will you do?'

'I shall travel.' Belinda gave a little laugh. 'Comfortably. I shall have a travelling carriage built. I shall go to the Low Countries, to Italy, to Turkey.'

'Foreign places?' Hannah sniffed. 'I prefer to see England.'

'And what of Scotland?'

'Full of savages in skirts.'

Belinda smiled. 'Nonetheless, I am determined to

remain cheerful. I shall endure the next two years planning my freedom.'

'We may have an adventure on the road to Bath.'

Belinda sighed. 'It is reputed to be the best road in the country. Oh, no. We shall travel sedately in this freezing cold and eventually we shall arrive, numb and miserable. I am sure my great-aunt considers fires in the bedchambers a sinful waste of money.'

Hannah looked out of the window. 'It is beginning to snow,' she said.

Light, feathery flakes were drifting down, dancing and spiralling. The sun had disappeared behind a bank of heavy grey cloud.

As the coach turned into the courtyard of another inn, the other passengers awoke. The dandified coachman, Hannah noticed with displeasure, had his hand out for tips before they were even seated round the table. He obviously did not think much of what he got, for he tossed the coins contemptuously in his hand before going off with the guard to the coachman's room.

'I do hope we will not land in a snow-drift,' said Mrs Judd nervously, as they were drinking the inevitable rum and hot milk and nutmeg. They were all so cold that even Miss Wimple did not protest when Belinda raised the tankard to her lips. It was customary for the gentlemen of the party on the stage-coach to pay for the ladies' refreshment. Mr Judd did not appear to find this courtesy necessary in this case, possibly because he was the only male passenger.

'We shall not come to any harm,' he said pompously. 'I shall see to that.'

'If it snows really hard,' said Mrs Judd, on whom the rum was having an invigorating effect, 'I do not know that you can do much about it.'

'I shall take the ribbons myself,' said her husband, quelling her with a frown. 'I have a pretty hand with the ribbons.'

'But I have only seen you drive a gig,' exclaimed his wife. 'Not a four-in-hand.'

He whispered something fiercely in her ear and she blushed, looked miserable, and said, 'Yes, dear.'

It was an unusually long stop. The waiter filled their tankards several times. The heat from a large roaring fire was thawing them all out and no one showed any signs of being anxious to be on the road again.

Then the coachman could be seen, lurching through the yard. He appeared, Hannah observed uneasily, to be very drunk. She began to wish there were more male passengers on board.

She took up a collection this time to tip the landlord to put hot bricks in the coach. Mr Judd demurred, but Mrs Judd opened her reticule and paid over some money, much to her husband's obvious fury.

She knows he don't like to tick her off too much in front of an audience, thought Hannah, and she's making the most of it.

As they all boarded the coach again, even Hannah began to feel sleepy. The coach rumbled on. There were three more stops that afternoon, and at each, hot drinks of brandy and rum and milk were served. Belinda requested hot lemonade and Hannah joined her in drinking it, noticing with amusement that the severe Miss Wimple was becoming tipsy. But her amusement died when she saw the state of the coachman. He could barely stand and had to be hoisted up on the box by the guard and a couple of ostlers.

Inside the coach again, Mrs Judd began to sing and was violently hushed by her husband, on whom alcohol had produced a morose effect.

'You are a fuddy-duddy,' said Mrs Judd with a laugh. She obviously liked the sound of the words because she kept repeating 'fuddy-duddy' over and over again and then tried 'duddy-fuddy,' all interspersed with laughs and hiccups.

Mr Judd sat huddled in his corner and glared at his wife. Hannah considered there was going to be one almighty marital row that evening when the Judds were in the seclusion of their bedchamber.

They finally rolled into Reading and found their rooms in the Bear and Bull. It was an expensive hostelry. Glad as she was of the comfort, Hannah began to wonder uneasily how long her inheritance would last. Five thousand pounds had seemed a fortune just a short time ago. But it was lovely to finally sink down on a feather bed with silk hangings and stretch out on lavender-scented sheets.

Her eyes were just beginning to close when she heard the sound of a thump from the next door, followed by a wail of pain.

Hannah sat up in bed.

The Judds were in that room next door. If a married man wanted to beat his wife, there was nothing she or anyone could do about it. But her heart went out to little Mrs Judd. There came the sound of another blow and then a thin, high wail of fear.

'For what I am about to do, God,' prayed Hannah Pym, 'please forgive me.'

She rose and dressed and went downstairs and ordered two tankards of mulled wine. She carried the steaming tankards up to her room. Throwing back the lid of her trunk, she took out a box in which she kept various medicines. Into one of the tankards, she poured a dose of laudanum.

She then carried the tray next door and knocked. Mr Judd in nightcap and dressing gown opened the door. Mrs Judd was a huddled, sobbing figure on the bed.

'I heard Mrs Judd cry out and was afraid she was suffering from nightmares. Is that the case?' demanded Hannah, steely eyed.

'Yes, yes,' said Mr Judd testily.

'I have brought you both some mulled wine,' said Hannah in governessy tones. 'It is the best thing to ensure a tranquil sleep and I shall stay here until you have both drunk it.'

She turned the tray deftly so that the drugged drink was nearest to Mr Judd. 'Thank you,' he said sourly. He was anxious to get back to the pleasures of tormenting his wife. He drained the tankard in one gulp and then took the tray from Hannah. 'I will take this to my wife,' he said. 'Good night.'

Hannah followed him into the room and neatly caught the tray as he began to weave and stumble.

'What the deuce?' he mumbled. He fell into an armchair beside the fire and began to snore.

Hannah walked over to the bed and patted Mrs Judd awkwardly on the shoulder. 'There, there,' she said. 'Do not cry any more. Your husband is asleep. Do not move him. He has had too much to drink.'

Mrs Judd sat up and dried her eyes. 'Thank you,' she whispered. 'I am very weak and silly . . . about nightmares, I mean.'

'Not silly at all,' said Hannah compassionately. 'Do try to sleep, Mrs Judd. We have a long journey tomorrow and perhaps a dangerous one if that wretched coachman don't sober up.'

'If only some highwayman would rise up from a hedgerow and shoot me,' said Mrs Judd drearily. She lay down and buried her face in the pillow. Hannah looked at her sadly and then went out and quietly closed the door.

2

I never had a piece of toast,
Particularly long and wide
But fell upon the sanded floor,
And always on the buttered side.

James Payn

When the passengers struggled back aboard The Quicksilver in a freezing black dawn, the snow was still falling steadily. But there was no wind. Wind was what caused accidents to stage-coaches, wind that hurled snow up into high drifts. Miss Wimple, rather red about the nose and eye after the libations of the day before, said the weather was all the fault of the government's encouraging balloonists. If God had meant us to fly, she insisted, he would have given us wings. It stood to reason that all these balloons bouncing into the clouds had disturbed the atmosphere and caused the snow to fall. Hannah's comment that she had never heard of a ballooning expedition in winter was treated with disdain.

Mr Judd sat groggily in his corner. His wife poured a little cologne in a handkerchief and bathed his brow; he smiled at her weakly and said he would never touch strong drink again.

'And neither will I,' declared Miss Wimple. 'And as for you, miss,' she went on, rounding on Belinda, 'you should never have had any in the first place.'

'At the latter stages yesterday,' said Belinda, 'Miss Pym and I were drinking lemonade, which is why we are the only two who look at all human this morning.'

'Do not address your elders in such a pert manner,' said Miss Wimple and then put a hand to her head and groaned as the guard tootled ferociously on the yard of tin and the coach moved off into the snow.

'I wonder how our coachman is faring this morning,' said Hannah.

'Disgraceful young churl,' commented Mr Judd wearily. 'He looked as if he had slept in his clothes.'

After Reading, the Bath road ran through flat pastoral country with barely a rise, past Sipson Green, where they changed horses again at the Magpie, and into Buckinghamshire, where it became broad, flat, and comfortable until Newbury. The day remained grey and threatening. There was no cheerful dawn, only the remorseless snow, which had begun to thicken. The horses had slowed to a walking pace. The bricks that had been placed on the floor of the coach that morning lost their heat and the miserable passengers began to shiver. Mr Judd lit the travelling lamp, not because he needed the light, but in the hope that it might disperse some of the biting cold.

'We should have more passengers inside to keep us warm,' said Hannah, trying to lighten the gloomy atmosphere when they alighted at the next stage. Everyone seemed to have forgotten the vow to give up strong drink, for every one of them was downing Nantes brandy like a trooper.

'Can be miserable, that can,' said the guard, a small, tough, wizened Cockney who had been passing their table and heard Hannah's remark. 'I mind when Jack Stacey was driving the Bath mail out o' London. Well, as you know, the mails can only take four inside and a tight squeeze it is. One night, when the mail was about to leave and was full, a gentleman who was a regular customer come up to Jack and insisted on getting in, for he had to get to Marlborough. Stacey held a council with the bookkeeper, observing that it wouldn't do to offend a regular. At last, the problem was solved by the gentleman jumping in just as the mail was leaving. What a squeeze that was. At the Bear at Maidenhead, where they changed the horses, Jack, he opens the coach door and says, "There's time for you to get a cup of coffee here, gentlemen, if you'd like to get out." No one moved, for, don't you see, they was fearful they wouldn't fit back in again. And they wouldn't budge at any of the other stages. Jack says they were all as silent as the grave and that's how they went on for seventy-four miles.'

'And how is our coachman today?' asked Hannah sharply.

26

'Tolrol',' said the guard with a grin. 'Flash Jack can handle the ribbons as good as any man in England, drunk *or* sober.'

'I would rather have him sober, *if* you don't mind,' said Hannah crossly. 'And is it not folly to travel on in this storm? If there are any ruts or obstacles in the road, he will not be able to see them.'

'Oh, all's right and tight, lady. No wind. Can't move when there's wind.'

Hannah sniffed and pulled her nose. Outside the leaded panes of the window lay a winter's scene. Snow sparkled on roads and roofs, lending beauty to the inn and to a jumble of Tudor houses. It would be pleasant, thought Hannah, to stay where they were and enjoy the view and wait until the snow stopped falling.

Dinner was served, a heavy inn dinner of roast beef, game pies, trifles and fruit. Hannah and Belinda drank lemonade, but Hannah noticed that Miss Wimple was drinking fortified wine, occasionally giving her lips genteel dabs with a lace handkerchief.

Reluctantly they all filed out again. Mr Judd was once more bullying his wife and she was doing everything she could to placate his temper, which, of course, only made it worse.

She should stand up to him, thought Hannah. It is that cringing, fluttering manner of hers. Such a manner brings out the beast in men. She remembered a chambermaid, Lucy, a shy, fair, pretty, fluffy girl. But she had had the same air as Mrs Judd and the butler was always shouting at her and the footmen seemed to delight in making her cry; even the lamp-boy put a dead rat in her bed. She was one of life's natural-born victims. Hannah, tired of fighting Lucy's battles, had found her work in the home of an elderly lady renowned for the sweetness of her temper.

But when she had called on Lucy on one of her rare days off, it was to find the girl red-eyed and broken in spirit. She said the other servants tormented her and her mistress shouted at her.

Hannah shook her head over the memory. It was amazing how fear encouraged bullying, as if the human race could smell it, like dogs.

'Do you read romances?' Belinda asked Hannah.

'No, I do not,' said Hannah roundly. 'A great deal of pernicious rubbish.'

Miss Wimple gave her an approving smile.

'Because,' went on Hannah and lost Miss Wimple's favour, 'what goes on in real life is more weird and wonderful than any romance.'

'How so?' asked Belinda, sensing a story.

Hannah settled her head comfortably against the squabs. 'Two miles out of Reading and on the right of the road', she said, 'is Calcott House. It was the home of Miss Kendrick, a rich and whimsical lady. There is a poem about this adventure, but I can only remember scraps of it. In any case, this Miss Kendrick had received many offers, all of which she refused, and it was reported she hated all men, when one day,

Being at a noble wedding
In the famous town of Reading,

28

> A young gentleman she saw
> Who belonged to the law.

'The young gentleman was Benjamin Child, Esquire. To him Miss Kendrick sent a challenge to a duel in Calcott Park. She did not assign any cause why Child – if such should prove to be his lot – should be skewered like a chicken. The barrister took the challenge seriously and turned up on the duelling ground, sword in hand. He found Miss Kendrick masked and waiting for him, also with a sword in her hand.

> "So now take your chance," says she,
> "Either fight or marry me."
> Said he, "Madam, pray what mean ye?
> In my life, I ne'er have seen ye."

'In fact, he suggested point-blank that she should unmask, not, perhaps, caring to take a pig in a poke. The lady, however, remained firm and incognito, when the intrepid Child, perhaps fortified with a view of the imposing Calcott House rising above the trees, told the lady he preferred to wed her rather than try her skill. Upon which, in the twinkling of an eye, he found himself

> Clothed in rich attire,
> Not inferior to a squire

– in fact, master of Calcott. And that all happened in 1712, less than an hundred years ago.'

'I would think you were making it all up,' said Belinda, 'except that the poetry is so bad. There is something so honest and worthy-sounding about bad poetry.'

'What is wrong?' asked Hannah sharply. Mrs Judd had begun to sob.

'Cease your caterwauling this instant,' snapped her husband.

'I h-have a p-premonition of disaster,' sobbed Mrs Judd.

'Fiddlesticks!' said Hannah, finding to her horror that she, too, was capable of being nasty to the inoffensive Mrs Judd.

'Well, I feel it. Here!'

She touched the region of her heart.

At that moment, the pace of the coach began to quicken. Hannah drew aside the red leather curtains, which she had drawn to shut out the vista of bleak snow. The snow was still falling thickly, but the horses were moving at a great rate.

She let down the window and, leaning out as far as she could, screwed up her eyes and tried to make out what was happening on the box. The coachman was hunched up, and with a sudden jolt of alarm Hannah noticed the reins had slipped from his hands.

'The coachman has fallen asleep,' she said. 'Someone has got to rouse him, or the guard.'

Mrs Judd screamed with alarm. Mr Judd opened his window and began to shout to the guard. The guard shouted something back and Mr Judd roared that the coachman had fallen asleep. They heard a thump on the roof as the guard moved from his seat at the back to join the coachman on the box.

Hannah hung out of the window again. The snow thinned slightly and she saw a curve of the road ahead.

Right across it, blocking the road, stood a hay wagon. She put up the window. 'We are for it!' she shouted. 'Down in the straw!' And Hannah crouched down on the floor of the carriage just as the coach swung off the road. They were thrown right and left. There were cries and sobs and swears and then the coach seemed to take flight. There was a short moment of silence and then, with an almighty crash, the whole coach landed in a river.

The Marquess of Frenton was riding along the marches of his estate. Despite the weather and the time of year, he considered it his duty to see that his property was not being neglected and that the high stone walls that bound the park had not been breached by either animals or humans.

He would not admit to himself that the real reason for the expedition was because of his house guests. With a view to choosing a bride, he had invited Miss Penelope Jordan and her parents, Sir Henry and Lady Jordan, to stay. He had danced with pretty Penelope several times during the Little Season in London. She was a stately brunette with cool, calm, chiselled features and moved with great elegance. She was very, very rich, or rather, her parents were, which meant she would come with a good dowry. Some

31

element of caution had prompted him to invite other house guests so as to make his motives not seem too obvious until he had fully made up his mind. But the other guests had not arrived, being stopped from travelling by the hard weather. It was not that he really had found Penelope any less suitable. The marquess was a fastidious man. He found her as elegant and well bred as ever. It was her parents' assumption that the knot was as good as tied that grated on him.

The marquess's late father had been a noisy, spend-thrift gambler and drunk. His mother's last words as she had followed her husband to the grave some four weeks later had been, 'Do not blame your father, my son. Men were ever thus.'

So the marquess at the age of twenty had found himself saddled with monstrous debts and a near ruin of a castle. He had worked hard and long, experimenting with new farming methods, taking what little capital he had and using it carefully on the stock exchange. The hostilities with the French had brought about a rise in the price of wheat, and slowly his fortunes began to turn. Now, at the age of thirty-four, he was a very wealthy man. His estates and farms were the envy of all less hard-working landowners. He had restored his ancestral home, Baddell Castle, to its long-forgotten glory. He loved fine statuary and fine paintings and the most delicate of china. His idea of a wife was someone who would grace his home like a work of art.

Hard physical labour in his younger years,

combined with a fastidious mind, had kept the more rampant lusts at bay. He had begun briefly to take pleasure when it was offered by, say, some fashionable widow at the London Season who knew very well what she was doing and did not have a heart to break. Succumbing to broken hearts, the marquess's observations had led him to believe, was something females were prone to do.

He was a tall man with a trim waist, square shoulders, and a lithe, athletic figure. He wore his hair powdered and confined at the nape of his neck with a ribbon. His face was high-nosed and rather stern and he had silvery-grey eyes that usually did not reflect what he was thinking.

He came to a wooded close overlooking the river Thrane that bordered his land. To his amazement, he saw a stage-coach coming down the opposite bank. A little guard was on the back of one of the horses and was hacking the traces free. The team of horses swerved right, clear of the careening coach. The coach wheels struck an outjutting ledge of rock. For one horrifying moment it sailed clear off the ledge and seemed to hang in the snowy air. And then it plunged straight down into the icy stretch of the river.

He dismounted and hurried down the bank, slithering and sliding until he reached the river. He sat down, pulled off his top-boots, and shrugged off his long black cloak, then waded into the icy torrent.

The carriage door swung open and a middle-aged lady with a rather crooked nose looked at him first in surprise and then relief.

'I see I shall not have to swim for it,' she said. 'The torrent seems shallow enough.'

The marquess made his way with difficulty to the coach and hung on to the open door. 'Climb on my back,' he ordered, 'and I will carry you to safety.'

'There is a lady here who is hurt,' said Hannah, for it was she. 'Take her first.'

'Very well,' said the marquess in a voice as cold and uncaring as the winter landscape. 'But be quick about it.'

'Help me,' said Hannah to Belinda as she stooped over Miss Wimple. That lady's face was an ugly colour and she had a great gash on her forehead.

They heaved and pushed at the inert Miss Wimple. 'Of what use are you?' cried Hannah furiously over her shoulder to Mr Judd, who was sitting on the floor of the coach.

'My wife has fainted,' he said sulkily.

'Pah!' retorted Hannah. 'Does such a little thing paralyse you? Had the coach not landed upright, we might all have been drowned.'

The marquess leaned into the carriage and managed to lift Miss Wimple in his arms. Hannah watched in admiration as he carried her easily to the bank and laid her down. Soon he was back again. By this time, Hannah had found her smelling salts. She held the bottle under Mrs Judd's nose and then slapped her face. 'Leave her alone,' cried Mr Judd, struggling to his feet.

'Then get you out of the carriage and carry your own wife to safety instead of letting that fine gentleman do all the work.'

Mr Judd looked weakly out of the door at the raging river. There was a moan behind him as his wife recovered from her faint.

'Now get down in the river,' commanded Hannah. 'No, sir,' she said to the marquess, 'stand aside. There is no reason why this gentleman cannot carry his own wife.'

Mr Judd dropped down into the river, lost his footing and fell into the water. The marquess swore and jerked him upright.

He backed up to the coach and his wife climbed on his back. She showed every sign of fainting again but was fully recovered to consciousness when her husband stumbled and tipped her into the river. The marquess fished her out and placed her on the bank next to Miss Wimple.

He turned around and saw with surprise that the middle-aged lady was crossing the river with a young girl on her back. He ran to help her.

'Shame on you,' he said to Belinda, 'to use this lady as a pack-horse.'

'I cannot stand on my ankle, sir,' said Belinda wrathfully. 'Do put me down, Miss Pym.'

The marquess drew on his boots and swung his cloak around his shoulders. He looked across the river. The guard and the coachman, who had been thrown clear, were leading the horses back up on to the road. The guard cupped his hands. 'Going to get help!' he shouted.

'Which means,' said Hannah, 'they are going to get drunk as soon as possible and forget all about us. That coachman was much too young for the job.'

The marquess stooped and lifted Miss Wimple in his arms. 'If the rest of you can make your way up the bank into the shelter of the trees, you may wait there until I bring carriages to bear you to safety. There is a road quite near.'

Hannah hitched Belinda's arm about her neck, Mr Judd helped his wife, and they all stumbled up the bank.

Once more Miss Wimple was laid down. The marquess mounted a great black horse and rode off.

'My clothes are freezing to me,' whispered Mrs Judd. 'I'm going to die and I know it.'

'Whoever that grand gentleman is, he is very competent,' said Hannah. 'We must all try to keep warm. We must walk up and down and stamp our feet and swing our arms and take turns at rubbing some warmth into Miss Wimple's limbs. Come along, everyone.'

Miss Pym was rather like a general, thought Belinda, amused despite her predicament, as Hannah beat her arms and stamped her feet and then knelt beside Miss Wimple and chafed her wrists.

After only a short time they heard the shouting of voices and rattling of wheels. Torches flickered through the trees, and then four men in outdoor livery appeared, followed by the marquess. Under his orders, two of them lifted Miss Wimple on to a stretcher and bore her off, one supported Belinda, and the other Mrs Judd.

'I have carriages waiting,' said the marquess to Hannah. 'Come quickly or you will catch the ague.'

As he bustled about, seeing them all into carriages, the marquess felt a momentary qualm. He should really have them driven to the nearest inn rather than inflict the passengers of the common stage on his guests. But their presence would give him a necessary breathing space, a wall to retreat behind while he considered his feelings for Penelope.

Hannah helped Belinda into one of the waiting carriages. She admired this lord, or whoever he was, immensely. He must have his staff well drilled to turn out so efficiently and promptly on a freezing night. She gave a happy smile and drew a huge bearskin rug up to her chin.

'Why, Miss Pym,' exclaimed Belinda, 'I declare you are actually enjoying a near escape from a freezing death.'

'It's an adventure,' said Hannah. 'Now, you see, my dear, it is better to look for romance in real life. Did you note how handsome our rescuer was?'

'I was too flustered and frightened and my ankle still hurts dreadfully,' said Belinda. 'He seemed very autocratic and severe and quite old. Where are we, I wonder?'

'I have a guidebook in my luggage,' said Hannah. 'Oh, dear, that wretched coachman has gone off with it.'

'Not he,' said Belinda. 'It had all fallen off the roof before we even hit the river and was strewn about the opposite bank.'

'Then our highly efficient host will collect it for us. We are travelling quite a way. Does he mean to deposit us all at some wayside inn?'

'No doubt.' Belinda shivered. 'I must get a physician immediately to look to poor Miss Wimple. How
came she to gash her forehead like that?'

'I think she was thrown against the lamp bracket.
How luxurious all this is, and what a great many
servants there seem to be.'

Outriders with flaming torches were riding alongside the carriages.

'We are slowing,' exclaimed Hannah. To the
shivering Belinda's dismay, she let down the glass and
leaned out. 'Oh, Miss Earle!' cried Hannah. 'You
have never seen the like.'

Curiosity overcoming cold, Belinda opened her
window and, clutching the edge for support to ease
her tortured ankle, she too leaned out.

The snow had stopped falling. In the lights of the
many torches and carriage lamps a great Norman
castle loomed up against the sky; battlements and
barbican, towers and turrets. They rolled slowly over
a wooden drawbridge and under two raised portcullises into a wide courtyard.

'Why have I never heard of this place?' said
Hannah, sitting down again. 'It is huge.'

'Have you visited many places?' asked Belinda.

Hannah shook her head. 'I have led a quiet and
sheltered life, like that of a nun. But I have read a great
deal, don't you see.'

The carriage rolled to a stop. A footman in green-
and-gold livery let down the steps and Hannah and
Belinda were assisted down.

The shivering stage-coach passengers were led into

the castle and all stood blinking in the sudden blaze of light. They found themselves in a great hall with a brown-and-white marble floor. A long refectory table with high-backed Jacobean chairs around it dominated the centre of the hall. There were battle flags and suits of armour and a long gallery running around the top of the hall to form an upper storey.

A house steward with his tall staff of office stood waiting.

'Convey our unexpected guests to the East Wing,' said the marquess. 'Send for the physician to attend us immediately. May I introduce myself? I am Frenton, the Marquess of Frenton, and you are now in my home, Baddell Castle, where I suggest you stay until I find out what has become of your coach. You are . . . ?'

Hannah stepped forward. 'I am Miss Hannah Pym of Kensington. May I present Miss Belinda Earle. Miss Wimple is the injured lady and Miss Earle's companion. Also, may I present Mr and Mrs Judd.'

The marquess turned to his steward and rapped out a bewildering, to Belinda, series of orders about which apartments were to be allotted to them.

Again, there were servants everywhere. Belinda clung nervously to Hannah, overawed by the magnificence of it all. They went up a broad staircase and along a bewildering multitude of passages. A house-keeper opened a door at last and said to Hannah, 'Your apartments are here, madam.' Oh, the joy of ex-housekeeper Hannah to hear herself called 'madam' by one of her own kind. 'You have a bedchamber as you go in and you will share a sitting-room with the young lady, who has a bedchamber on the other side. His lordship is sending up your trunks, which the men rescued from the side of the river. The footmen will carry up your baths in a trice.'

Hannah looked around the apartment in satisfaction. The walls were papered with a heavy red paper. The great four-poster bed had dull red silk hangings. The fireplace was Queen Anne and as unlovely a piece of architecture as anything attributed to that poor lady's name. It had a heavy overmantel that almost dwarfed the grate beneath. But there was a bright fire burning.

She helped Belinda through a pretty sitting-room decorated in the Chinese manner and into a bedroom where blue silk, blue wallpaper, and a four-poster bed and fire-place copied the red room in everything but colour.

Their trunks were brought in, followed very quickly by the baths, which were filled by the footmen, and then the two ladies were left in peace.

Hannah sat in the bath in front of the fireplace, carefully holding the guidebook clear of the water. 'I have found it,' she called through the open door to Belinda. 'Baddell Castle. Ah, it used to belong to the Earls of Jesper. The last earl died in 1590 without children, his estates escheated to the Crown, and all the court rolls and records went to London and disappeared in the middle of the seventeenth century, so it was a castle without much history that anyone knows of or ghosts or what have you, so everyone forgot about it. It says that the present owner, the Marquess of Frenton, repels visitors.'

'I am glad he did not repel us,' called Belinda.

'The Crown gave the first Marquess of Frenton the castle and estates.'

'What shall I wear?' asked Belinda. 'If we are to dine here, we could dine in our undress.'

'I think we should dress for a formal supper, just in case.'

'The marquess is hardly likely to ask coach passengers to sit down with him,' protested Belinda.

'He did not need to take us into his home,' Hannah pointed out. 'He could have left us at some inn.'

As soon as they had bathed and dressed, servants appeared to remove the baths, and then a physician made his entrance. He said that Miss Wimple was still unconscious but he had hopes she would soon recover. He then examined Belinda's ankle and confirmed that it was a bad sprain and strapped it up.

Then a lady's maid came in. She said she was called Betty. Hannah thought it quite likely that she had some other name, for employers very frequently called their lady's maids Betty.

Hannah enjoyed the luxury of having her hair done and her large shawl arranged tastefully on her shoulders. Then, while Belinda's hair was being arranged, Hannah asked the maid, 'When you have finished, can you take us to Miss Wimple? She is the lady who has suffered a bad accident.'

The maid nodded, and after she had dressed Belinda's fine hair in one of the new Grecian styles, she led them out and along the corridor and into Miss Wimple's bedchamber.

Miss Wimple was lying like one dead. Hannah felt her forehead and found it hot. A little chambermaid was piling logs on the fire. 'The doctor said she would live,' said the chambermaid.

A footman appeared in the doorway. 'His lordship's compliments,' he said. 'You are to follow me.'

'I will stay here,' said Hannah firmly.

'Beg pardon, madam,' said the footman. 'Mrs James, the housekeeper, will soon be here to sit with the poor lady, and she will let you know as soon as there is any change.'

Belinda and Hannah followed him out, back along a chain of corridors, and then down the main staircase to the first floor. 'His lordship is in the Cedar Room,' said the footman, and flung open the double doors.

Belinda hesitated nervously in the doorway until Hannah gave her a little push.

The Cedar Room was enormous. The cedar-wood panelling which gave it its name was hung with family portraits. Huge chandeliers hung from the ornately designed ceiling. There was a large Adam fireplace in the centre of the opposite wall, and a French carpet covered the floor.

Huge windows had thick velvet curtains with heavy swags of fringe drawn against the winter's night. The gigantic area of the room was dotted about with little islands of tables and chairs.

At the island nearest the fireplace sat a very beautiful lady and a middle-aged couple.

The marquess was standing by the fireplace. He was wearing an evening coat of dark-blue watered silk with a high collar and a ruffled shirt. His breeches of the same material were fastened at the knee with gold buckles. His silk stockings were of gold-and-white stripes and his black shoes had gold buckles. He had a fine sapphire in the snowy folds of his cravat and a large square sapphire ring on his finger.

Hannah shot a covert glance at Belinda and was glad that young lady was looking every bit as finely dressed as the marquess's guests.

She was wearing a gown of pale lilac satin and a fine necklace of amethysts set in old gold. She had lilac silk heelless slippers to match with ribbons crossed across the ankles, and, on her arms, long gloves of lilac kid. Hannah had put on a fine and delicate muslin cap. She knew the Norfolk shawl about her shoulders was of the finest quality, as was her plum-coloured silk gown with matching silk gloves.

The marquess approached Belinda and Hannah, his eyes narrowing a little in surprise, for there was no denying the richness of the ladies' gowns. He wondered briefly what they had been doing travelling on the stage.

He introduced them to Miss Penelope Jordan and her parents. Mr and Mrs Judd made their entrance, Mrs Judd clinging tightly to her husband's arm. Belinda saw a mocking smile curving Penelope's lips and the teasing look she threw the marquess as if to say, 'My dear, what people!'

All in that moment, Belinda found herself disliking Penelope very much indeed.

The Judds were plainly and respectably dressed. But Mrs Judd's gown was of an old-fashioned cut and Mr Judd was in morning dress, not having brought any evening dress with him, which, thought Belinda crossly, was perfectly understandable. She flashed a contemptuous look at Penelope and then realized the marquess was watching her and blushed faintly.

A butler and two footmen entered bearing trays of hot negus for the ladies and decanters of wine for the men.

All sat down on chairs arranged for them in a circle in front of the fire. Belinda sipped her negus and covertly studied the Jordans. Sir Henry Jordan was fat and florid with a jovial manner belied by the hardness of a pair of small brown eyes. Lady Jordan showed traces of an earlier beauty in thick, luxuriant, if grey-streaked hair, a statuesque figure, and large brown eyes. But little lines of discontent had caused her mouth to set in a permanent droop and two heavy vertical lines caused by frowning marred her forehead.

'Why are you travelling on the stage, Miss Earle?' demanded Penelope, her eyes flicking over the splendour of Belinda's gown.

'To get to The Bath,' said Belinda calmly.

'I would have thought you would have preferred to travel in your own carriage,' pursued Penelope.

Seized with a mischievous desire to lower her social status to that of the Judds, Belinda said airily, 'My family do not own a carriage.' She turned to the marquess. 'All my concern is for Miss Wimple, my poor companion.'

'I have told the physician to return within the hour,' said the marquess. 'He will stay here for the night and so be available to help when he is required.'

'Thank you, my lord. You are so very kind.' Belinda's face suddenly lit up in a charming smile. The marquess smiled back, oddly intrigued by this young lady with the wispy-fine slate-coloured hair and the wicked-looking sensual mouth.

'You have a very fine place here, my lord,' said Mr Judd nervously.

'It'll be something to tell your grandchildren, hey?' said Sir Henry, all mock joviality. 'I wager you never thought, considering your social station, to be the guest of an earl.'

Belinda winced and Hannah's lips clamped tightly together in disapproval. How quaint, thought Penelope, amused. These upstarts of the stage-coach actually consider that Papa is being vulgar. But then she saw the chilly, calculating way in which the marquess was regarding her father and felt a stab of unease.

The marquess rose to escort them to supper. Penelope's feeling of unease grew, for the marquess placed Belinda on his right hand and Hannah on his left. Moreover, the long dining-table had been replaced by a round one. The marquess had not liked the way Penelope had automatically taken the opposite end of the long table from him as if she were already established as his wife, and so had ordered the round table and had had it delivered that very day.

Penelope's beautiful eyes narrowed as they surveyed Belinda. There was something definitely odd about that young woman. Her arrival on the scene seemed just too opportune. Perhaps she had engineered the accident, thought Penelope pettishly, not stopping to consider that the idea of any young lady causing a coach to crash down in an icy river in the faint hope that the marquess would come riding by was stupid in the extreme.

Penelope had been told from her earliest days that she was beautiful beyond compare. She had practised a certain elegance of manner but had stopped there at improvement, considering her looks enough to contribute to any company.

Belinda, on the other hand, had assiduously practised the art of conversation to make up for what she felt was her own lack of attractions. She turned to the marquess and began to speak.

3

Damn with faint praise, assent with civil leer,
And without sneering teach the rest to sneer;
Willing to wound, and yet afraid to strike,
Just hint a fault and hesitate dislike.

Alexander Pope

'It is most generous of you, my lord,' said Belinda, 'to provide us with shelter and accommodation.'

'My pleasure, I assure you, Miss Earle. Do you reside with family in The Bath?'

'I am to stay with Great-Aunt Harriet.'

'And shall you make your come-out there?'

'I have already made my come-out, my lord, at the last Season. I am now going "in" again.'

He looked at her curiously. 'And why is that?' Belinda hesitated while vermicelli soup was served. She was aware of Penelope's eyes resting on her, and somehow aware that Penelope's shell-like ears were straining to catch every syllable. She must not tell this marquess or anyone about the footman. Who would understand, except perhaps someone like the odd Miss Pym? To say one had run away with a footman suggested a world of unladylike passion. 'I did not take,' she said calmly. 'I am lucky to be only travelling as far as The Bath. I could just as well have been sent to India or to some battlefront in hope that my not-too-obvious charms might catch the eye of a homesick member of the East India Company or some war-weary soldier.'

'You are very frank,' commented the marquess, feeling sure he should disapprove of any lady who openly ran down her own attractions and appearance, and yet finding in himself an odd desire to instil some much-needed vanity into Miss Earle. 'You should not disparage yourself,' he pointed out. 'People will take you at your own valuation. If you go about saying openly, "I am not attractive," then you will, I may say, find that people think you so. Which would be a pity.'

'How so?' demanded Belinda, her eyes dancing.

'They might then fail to notice that your figure is good and your eyes very fine.'

Belinda should have blushed and lowered her eyes. Instead she looked at him in open gratitude. 'Do you really think so?' she asked. Then her face fell. 'But of course you do not. You are merely flirting with me as a matter of form.'

'I never flirt,' said the marquess frostily.

'Do you not? I *long* to be able to flirt with ease, but I have an unfortunate habit of telling the truth. Not *all* the truth all of the time, don't you see, for if you asked me if I were enjoying myself at present, I would be obliged to say, "Yes," for it would be churlish to say else.'

'Obviously then you are not enjoying yourself. What is wrong? You may speak freely. Your honesty amuses me.'

'Well ... well, it is just that I sense you have offended your guests by expecting them to dine with passengers from the stage.'

He stiffened. 'My guests have too much breeding to betray either like or dislike.'

'Unlike me, you see what you want to see.' Belinda lowered her voice. 'Regard how dainty Mrs Judd takes little sips of soup with a hand that trembles with nerves. Miss Jordan is aware of her discomfort and so she stares at her openly – that is, when she is not straining to hear what we are saying – in the hope of making her feel worse. Sir Henry and Lady Jordan maintain an icy silence.'

He had promised not to be offended, but he found he was becoming very angry with her indeed. 'In that case,' he said coldly, 'I suggest you turn your attention to Mr Judd on your other side and I shall devote myself to Miss Pym.

As he turned away, he heard Belinda mutter, 'I should have known you would be angry.'

The soup had been removed and fried whitebait was being served.

Hannah's sharp ears had heard most of the inter-change between the marquess and Belinda. She felt

49

impatient with that young lady. If that was how she had gone on during her Season, then no wonder she had not found any suitable beaux.

'Are you a friend of Miss Earle?' She realised the marquess was asking her.

'I am now, my lord,' said Hannah. 'But it is a friendship of very short duration, having only started when I joined the coach.'

'I understand that you like to travel, Miss Pym?'

'Oh, so very much,' said Hannah. 'It is an excellent way of meeting people.'

'Odso! I was given to understand that although a variety of classes travel together on the stage, they hardly ever exchange a common civility.'

'True,' agreed Hannah. 'But this is such an adventure.' Her large strange eyes, which changed colour according to her mood, glowed green with excitement.

'But wading through an icy river in winter is most people's idea of hell rather than a gay adventure, Miss Pym.'

'I am very tough,' said Hannah. 'I only hope the same can be said for poor Miss Wimple, and Mrs Judd is not at all strong in spirit.'

'Have you always travelled?'

'Oh, no, my lord. I always dreamt of it, but it did not become possible until this year, when I received a legacy from a relative. I plan to go the length and breadth of England. This is a wonderful castle. I thought such piles as this would have fallen into ruins.'

'It amuses me to maintain it in its original splendour, on the outside at least,' said the marquess. 'I do not think I should find stone-flagged floors covered with rushes inside at all comfortable. But you do not take wine, Miss Pym.'

'Although I have a great deal of stamina,' said Hannah, 'I fear, after the exhaustion caused by the recent accident, that wine would go straight to my head. The negus before supper was enough, I thank you.'

The marquess glanced across Hannah to where Belinda was making an obvious effort to put Mr Judd at his ease. Mr Judd, it appeared, was a music teacher at a ladies' seminary in Bath. Belinda was saying teasingly that he must break the hearts of all his young ladies, and Mr Judd was growing visibly more expansive and swell-headed. For a young lady who claimed she did not know how to flirt, she was doing very well, reflected the marquess. He was aware that the Jordans were sitting in icy silence and felt impatient with them. He would expect, in any wife he chose, the same ease of manner with his tenants as with his peers. But the candle-light played softly on the whiteness of Penelope's arms and on the glossy tresses of her hair and instead of blaming her for her cold behaviour, he felt obscurely it was all this Miss Earle's fault. He could not, for example, possibly contemplate marriage to any female as farouche as Miss Earle. One would never know what to expect from her from one moment to the next. And on that thought followed another, treacherous one: that it was very boring to know exactly what anyone would say and do from one moment to the other.

'I heard Miss Earle tell you she is being sent to Bath because she did not "take" at her last Season,' said Hannah. 'I find that most strange. She is a great heiress and has an openness and liveliness of mind I find enchanting.'

'I did not think great heiresses ever remained unwed,' said the marquess.

'Miss Earle had several offers, but her aunt and uncle, who strike me as rather pushing sorts of people, were hanging out for a title.'

'If her aunt and uncle are indeed very wealthy, why do they send her on the stage? Miss Earle did say they did not possess their own carriage.'

'Do you know, I really think she was being mischievous when she said that. I happen to know that to be untrue. She arrived at the coaching inn in a very fine equipage.'

'I cannot see why she should choose to lie.'

Hannah pulled her nose in embarrassment. The answer was that she felt sure Belinda had pretended to be on a social level with, say, the Judds in order to tease the Jordans.

She smiled at the marquess instead and turned to Sir Henry, who was on her other side. 'I do hope Miss Wimple, Miss Earle's companion, recovers soon so that we may continue our journey,' said Hannah.

Sir Henry maintained a stony silence.

The marquess's voice sounded sharp and clear. 'Miss Pym has just said something to you, Sir Henry. Are you become deaf? Would you like me to repeat it for you?'

Sir Henry looked startled and then rallied. 'Wits were wandering. Fact is, Miss Pym, I don't know Miss Wimple, so it follows that I do not have any interest in her welfare.'

The marquess's silvery-grey eyes shone with a frosty light. Good heavens, thought Penelope, this Miss Pym is outmanoeuvring us. Somehow, she is cleverly managing to make poor Papa look vulgar and unfeeling. Frenton obviously expects us to be civil to these commoners. What an odd fancy! But if I do not play my cards aright, he will take me in dislike as well.

She turned to Mrs Judd and said gently, 'I fear you must be feeling fatigued after your experience. How shocking for you. You must have feared for your life.'

Mrs Judd blushed at the sudden attention and said in a faint voice that she was feeling overset. Hannah shrewdly judged that the gamecock on her plate with which Mrs Judd was struggling was upsetting her more than her dousing in the river. It showed a tendency to skid across her plate as she strove to a cut a piece from it.

'Would you be so good,' said Hannah to the marquess, 'as to ask your butler to carve the gamecock for us ladies. I fear we lack the dexterity to tackle it ourselves.'

The marquess called the butler forward and Mrs Judd flashed Hannah a grateful look as the bird was removed and then brought back to her, carved into manageable pieces. But the peas were another matter. Attacking peas with a two-pronged fork was a difficult job at the best of times. She decided to leave them alone.

The marquess apologized for the scanty fare, saying it was only a light supper as they had already had dinner, but urged them all to order anything else they wished. Unlike Belinda and Hannah, who knew to take only a little of what was offered, the Judds had filled their plates at each course and now felt they had never eaten such huge quantities of food.

Finally the cover was removed and nuts and fruit were placed on the table, along with a trolley on wheels that contained decanters of madeira, canary, port and brandy. The trolley was in the shape of a sailing ship with silver sails and gold rigging. Belinda glanced about the room – at the elegance of the Adam fireplace, the Aubusson carpet, the paintings of still life, the green-and-gold damask curtains at the windows and at the sage-green silk-upholstered dining-chairs – and then back at that sailing ship. It seemed out of place, a vulgar piece of nonsense, a rich man's toy.

'Glad to see you've put it to use, Frenton,' said Sir Henry expansively, indicating the trolley.

'It was a most generous present,' murmured the marquess.

There were many wax candles burning in the room and wax candles on the dining-table. The marquess was half turned away from Belinda, talking to Hannah. Belinda noticed that his white-powdered hair showed glints of red in the light and felt strangely reassured. Red hair was very unfashionable and she was glad to find there was something human and unfashionable about this rather intimidating man.

As if conscious of her gaze, he turned abruptly and found her staring at his hair. 'Is anything the matter?' he demanded sharply.

Belinda was too tired to do other than tell the truth. To Hannah's dismay, she heard Belinda reply, 'It's your hair. It is red.'

'If you mean my hair is not sufficiently powdered, then say so,' snapped the marquess.

'It is not that,' said Belinda, wandering deeper into the thicket of bad social behaviour. 'Red, don't you see. Such an unfashionable colour.'

His lips tightened in disapproval as he turned back to Hannah.

Now Belinda wished this interminable supper would end. Her ankle had begun to ache again. She looked hopefully towards Lady Jordan, whose duty it was, surely, to rise to her feet and lead the ladies back to the Cedar Room and leave the gentlemen to their wine.

But it was the marquess who suggested they repair to the Cedar Rooni, and so they all rose together. The marquess led the way with Penelope on his arm, Sir Henry and Lady Jordan followed, then Hannah and Belinda, with the Judds bringing up the rear.

The confidence she had experienced during the earlier part of the meal deserted Belinda. She felt plain and gauche. Somehow, it was the Jordans' bad behaviour that had given her courage. But now Penelope was being gracious to the Judds, and her parents, who seemed to take their lead from their beautiful daughter, were following her example. As

Penelope noticed Belinda's crushed mien, so her graciousness and courtesy grew. She begged Mr Judd to entertain them if he was not too tired, and Mr Judd, flushed with all this exalted attention, gladly agreed. He walked to a pianoforte that stood against the far wall and, flexing his hands like a concert pianist, sat down and began to play. Belinda had expected him to play a virtuoso piece in an effort to impress, but he played a selection of sentimental ballads and then he began to sing. So that's what the attraction is, thought Hannah, looking at Mrs Judd's radiant face. Mr Judd played beautifully and had a rich tenor voice.

Belinda listened enthralled, resting her chin on her hand, her eyes dreamy. Gone was her recent unease and depression. She had dreamt before only of freedom, freedom to live her own life, freedom from marriage. But as the liquid, sentimental music coiled around her, she dreamt for almost the first time of a lover, a merry man full of laughter who would be a companion on her travels.

Penelope, who was tone-deaf, sat like a classical statue with her mouth in the same little curved smile and her eyes as blank.

The marquess leaned back in an armchair and stretched out his buckled shoes to the blaze. He looked with admiration at Penelope, at the lines of her body, at the proud set of her head, and then, almost despite himself, his gaze was drawn to Belinda.

Her eyes were full of dreams, and her wispy, baby-fine hair gave her an elfin look. That splendidly passionate mouth of hers was in repose, just waiting for a kiss . . .

He gave himself a mental shake. The evening had turned out very pleasant after all. Judd was a superb performer. Penelope was behaving just as she ought. Mrs Judd looked happy and at ease for the first time. She was a dainty little thing, thought the marquess, despite her unfashionable gown. Her fair hair was dressed in ringlets and her wide eyes were pale blue and her skin was fine and delicate. When Mr Judd ceased playing for a moment, the marquess asked her, 'Do you sing as well, Mrs Judd? It would give me great pleasure to hear you.'

Belinda expected Mrs Judd to blush and disclaim but she rose and walked quietly to the piano and stood beside her husband. She began to sing 'Cherry Ripe'. Belinda sat up straight, her eyes wide with amazement. Mrs Judd had a beautiful soprano voice, as clear as a bell.

What a pair of nightingales! thought the marquess. And what are they doing hidden away in a ladies' seminary in Bath?

Only Hannah and Penelope remained unmoved; Penelope because music meant nothing to her, good or bad, and Hannah because her mind was busy with plans. Mrs Judd was eminently bullyable. But what was it that started friction in a marriage? Why, debt, lack of money, thought Hannah with satisfaction. Rows began and went on. Mr Judd was a weak man and in a perverse way had begun to enjoy ill-treating his wife. The crushable Mrs Judd had begun to sink under such treatment and, thinking little of herself, obscurely felt she deserved it, which, in a woman, was an open invitation for more bad treatment.

Before leaving her husband, Mrs Clarence, wife of Hannah's late employer, had held a musicale in Thornton Hall, their home in Kensington. Ever considerate of the servants, she had arranged for the staff to listen outside the room in which the concert was being held. A couple of singers, man and wife, had been engaged at great expense. But they had not been nearly so good as the Judds, thought Hannah. Something must be done about them. It was no use saying Mrs Judd would be better off without that husband of hers. Women like Mrs Judd would simply go ahead and find another bully. They need a patron, thought Hannah, eyeing the marquess covertly. That gentleman was sitting enraptured by the singing, his normally austere face looking younger. He and Belinda looked similar in that moment, each wrapped up in the pleasure of the music.

They must marry.

Hannah gave a little sigh. She had set herself a great task, but she was determined that if Hannah Pym had any say in the matter, then Belinda Earle would arrive in Bath as an engaged lady.

The song was finished. The marquess, despite his absorption, had nonetheless sensed that it was Belinda, not Penelope, who had shared his pleasure in the singing and music.

Hannah decided to retire and have a good night's

sleep while she made her plans. She usually needed very little sleep, but the bitter cold of the day and the alarms of the accident had left her feeling tired. Belinda rose at the same time, curtsied to the company, and followed Hannah from the room. The Judds, too, made their escape.

'An unexpectedly charming evening,' said Penelope. 'It is very educational to study people of a rank lower than oneself.'

'I think you will find Miss Earle is of our rank in life,' said the marquess. Having been toadied to and then pursued by adventurers and wastrels from an early age, he had developed a nice eye for social distinctions. 'In fact, I know I have heard the name before. Untitled aristocracy, I believe.'

'Are you sure?' cooed Penelope. 'Miss Earle is a delightful creature and I quite dote on her already, but a little strange in her ways, do you not think? A certain gaucherie? I could not help but overhear what she said to you at supper. To remark on the colour of a gentleman's hair! I declare I was shocked. But she has been badly brought up perhaps.'

The marquess should have agreed because he did feel that Miss Earle was regrettably outspoken, but some imp of perversity prompted him to say, 'I find her inoffensive and much to be pitied. Miss Pym assures me she is an heiress. I can only think it reprehensible that her uncle and aunt found it necessary to subject her to the rigours of a stage-coach in winter.'

He studied the toes of his shoes while the Jordans

exchanged startled glances. This Belinda Earle must be sent on her way as soon as possible.

Belinda and Hannah made their way to Miss Wimple's room. The physician, a Dr Patterson, was bending over the bed, shaving Miss Wimple's head. Belinda let out a cry of alarm. 'It is the necessary treatment for concussion,' said the doctor, pausing in his work. 'I shall then apply leeches to her head. After that, I shall apply this salve, which is made with half an ounce of sal ammoniac, two tablespoons of vinegar, and the same quantity of whisky in half a pint of water. Then Miss Wimple, should she show any signs of regaining consciousness, will be given a pill made from five grains of camomile and some quantity of antimonial powder with a little breadcrumb. Do not fear, ladies. I am persuaded Miss Wimple is of a strong constitution.'

The ladies edged out of the room, retreating backwards as if before royalty, so grand and imperious was Dr Patterson's manner. Once back in their own sitting room, Belinda began to giggle. 'Poor Miss Wimple. She will be outraged when she comes to her senses and finds she is as bald as a coot.'

Betty, the lady's maid, entered, but Hannah dismissed her, saying they would make themselves ready for bed.

'Rather high-handed of you,' said Belinda crossly when Betty had left. 'Now I shall have to untie the tapes of my gown myself and brush my own hair.'

'You are quite able to brush your hair yourself, and

I shall help you with your gown. What if you were up the Amazon River or somewhere monstrous interesting like that? You could not expect a lady's maid to be on hand.'

'True, but if I and everyone else decided to do without lady's maids, there would be a great number of unfortunate servants left unemployed.'

'But I want to talk to you,' said Hannah. 'I *have* to talk to you.'

'What about?' demanded Belinda, stifling a yawn.

'Have you noticed the Marquess of Fenton?'

'Of course I have. A very kind host.'

'He is a handsome man.'

Belinda scratched her head in an unladylike way. Then she laughed. 'Why, Miss Pym, you are like all the rest. If a man has a title and a fortune, then of course he is handsome.'

'I think you are both well suited,' said Hannah.

'My dear Miss Pym, your wits are addled with fatigue. The man must be in his thirties. He is very cold and austere. Did you mark the fine paintings, the *objets d'art*? That is what he loves. He will probably wed this Miss Jordan and add her to his collection.'

'But he is fastidious, and she is not very clever, I think, and has no gentility of manner,' said Hannah eagerly. 'I tell you this because I was alarmed to hear the openness of your speech at supper. You must never tell him about the footman.'

'Of course not. I am not such a widgeon. Ladies who run away with servants are always credited with having vulgar and lustful passions. Probably the ladies were simply bored to tears.'

'You may have the right of it,' said Hannah sadly. 'Poor Mrs Clarence.'

'Who was Mrs Clarence?'

'I shall be open with you. I am but lately risen to the ranks of gentility. For years I was a servant in the Clarence household at Thornton Hall in Kensington.'

'Tell me about it,' said Belinda, brightening at the prospect of a story.

'I was taken from the orphanage when I was very young and sent to Thornton Hall as a scullery maid. Mr and Mrs Clarence were newly-weds. I was very fortunate. The house was warm, and there was food to eat, which could not be said about the orphanage. It was a happy household. Most ladies never see the inside of their own kitchens, but not Mrs Clarence. She was so pretty and gay.' Hannah sighed. 'Mr Clarence was a good man but very withdrawn and morose. At first Mrs Clarence got her way and there were plenty of parties and balls and picnics, and occasionally we servants were allowed to go to the play. I worked very hard and became between-stairs maid, then housemaid, then first housemaid, and then my greatest ambition was realized, and I was made housekeeper. I was competent, but my work was not so arduous, and I had more time to realize that the Clarences were not happy. A few parties were still held, but Mr Clarence would cast gloom over every assembly. And then, one day, Mrs Clarence ran away with one of the footmen. It was a shock to us all. She had not seemed to favour him overmuch. It was considered that passion had got the better of breeding, but now I wonder. I could see her beauty fading and her high spirits being worn down under her husband's moodiness and disapproval. The footman was a happy young man, very cheerful and good-natured. But the world still thinks ill of Mrs Clarence and assumes she died soon after in disgrace. But she was a wealthy woman in her own right, so they would not starve. I would like to find her again and tell her that her husband is dead, and that she is free to marry, but I do not know where she can be found.

'Mr Clarence died and left me a legacy. How I longed to be free to travel in those long years during which he became a recluse.'

'Why did you stay?' asked Belinda curiously.

'I was loyal. I never managed to save much money. I ran the house my own way. I could perhaps have moved to a livelier household, but might have been badly treated by some new mistress. But as to your future, miss, would it not be better to be mistress of this grand castle and a marchioness than to go to Bath in disgrace?'

Belinda rose to her feet and stooped and dropped a kiss somewhere in the air above Hannah's head. 'Dear Miss Pym,' she said with a laugh. 'I shall endure my stay with Great-Aunt Harriet and dream of my future as a spinster. You need not help me to bed. I am not really such a spoilt brat that I cannot look after myself.'

Hannah took herself off to her own bedroom. She chided herself for having been too forward too soon.

Belinda obviously did not view the marquess with a loverlike eye and probably never would.

The marquess said good night to the Jordans and mounted the stairs. He decided to see how Miss Wimple was faring. He was startled at that lady's shaven head, and then realized she had probably been leeched. The doctor was holding a glass to her lips, as she had just regained consciousness.

'I am very pleased with our patient's progress, my lord,' said Dr Patterson.

'I see she has recovered her senses.' The marquess approached the bed. 'You have finished leeching the lady's head. It might be a good idea to tie a nightcap on her.'

'Just about to do that,' said the doctor. A maid appeared from the shadowy recesses of the bedroom, stooped over Miss Wimple and tied on a lacy nightcap, and then collected the empty glass from the doctor and left the room.

'When will she be fit to travel?' asked the marquess.

'Hard to tell. A week. Two weeks. Of course, if these passengers weary you, they could be conveyed to the Queen Bess within, say, a couple of days. As you know, my lord, it is an excellent hostelry, not far from here, and our patient could be taken there lying in one of your carriages.'

'We shall see,' said the marquess. 'You may retire for the night, Doctor. I shall wait with the patient until a servant arrives to watch over her. Ask the

64

housekeeper for a suitable maid. She herself has done her stint of duty at the bedside.'

The doctor left. Miss Wimple appeared to be trying to speak. The marquess drew even closer to the bed. 'Belinda – Miss Earle?' whispered Miss Wimple in a weak voice.

'She is safe and well, madam. Your only concern is to regain your health.'

'Wayward girl,' said Miss Wimple in a stronger voice. 'You are the Marquess of Frenton, Dr Patterson tells me.'

'At your service, ma'am.'

'My compliments to your wife, my lord.'

'I am not married.'

'Ah. You must, my lord, forgive my charge's wayward ways. Running off with a footman indeed.'

Miss Wimple's voice was becoming stronger by the minute.

'Ran off with a footman, did she?' asked the marquess.

'Nothing came of it.' Miss Wimple's voice became suddenly weary. 'A wicked, wicked girl, but even the footman did not want her.' Her voice trailed away and her eyelids began to droop.

And having successfully demolished Belinda's reputation in the eyes of the Marquess of Frenton, Miss Wimple folded her hands on her massive bosom and fell asleep.

4

There's something undoubtedly in a fine air,
To know how to smile and be able to stare,
High breeding is something, but well-bred or not,
In the end the one question is, what have you got.
So needful it is to have money, heigh-ho!
So needful it is to have money.

Arthur Hugh Clough

Belinda awoke and for a short moment did not know where she was. Then recollection came flooding back. She was in Baddell Castle, a guest of the Marquess of Frenton. She thought with amusement about Miss Pym's ambitions for her. Almost as bad as Aunt and Uncle, reflected Belinda. How they would disgrace themselves were they both here, primping me and pushing me forward.

Her stomach gave an unladylike rumble. She wondered whether she could expect breakfast or if the marquess kept London hours and rose about two in the afternoon. Her stomach rumbled again and she threw back the covers, climbed down from the high bed, pulled on a wrapper, and went in search of Miss Pym. That lady's bed was empty, so Belinda decided to dress and go downstairs.

She rang the bell to summon the lady's maid and spent an enjoyable half-hour choosing an ensemble. Belinda had had little interest in clothes in London and would not admit to herself that this sudden desire to be fashionably gowned was to compete with Penelope Jordan.

She chose a cambric muslin gown, white with a small blue velvet spot and with a pelisse of blue silk trimmed with fur to wear over it. For her head, she selected the newest style in caps, a confection of muslin with the same blue velvet spot as her gown. Olive-green stockings, the very latest colour, were chosen as they, or rather one of them, would be seen, fashion demanding that any *elegante* should loop her gown over one arm to show one leg almost to the knee.

Betty, the maid, heated the curling tongs and arranged Belinda's hair in a simple but flattering style before putting the froth of a cap on top of it.

On leaving the warmth of the bedroom where the fire had been burning brightly, Belinda was struck by the chill of the corridor. Through a mullioned window she could see snow falling steadily on the battlements. Both portcullises were lowered. It was amazing that they were still in use. Obviously the marquess did not expect or did not desire any further visitors.

She hesitated at the top of the main staircase and looked about for a servant to guide her to the breakfast room. She began to wonder if breakfast was being served at all. It was only eight in the morning, and a disgracefully unfashionable hour for any lady to be up and about. But Betty had made no comment, and surely the maid would have said something.

Then she saw a footman ascending the staircase and went down to meet him. To her query, he inclined his powdered head and said, 'Follow me, miss.' He led the way down to the first landing and then along a passage and threw open the door of a room.

To Belinda's relief, the sideboard was laden with dishes. She sat down at a small mahogany table. The butler came in carrying a tray with pots of coffee, tea and hot chocolate, but asked her if she would prefer beer. Belinda asked for tea and then chose kidneys, bacon, egg and toast. She marvelled at the efficiency of the marquess's staff, who could produce all this food so quickly, but no sooner had she begun to eat than the door opened and the marquess came in. Breakfast had been prepared for him, and he had not expected any of his guests to be up so early, for he looked at her in surprise.

He had obviously come in from riding, for he was wearing top-boots, leather breeches, a black coat, and a ruffled shirt. His hair was unpowdered and was indeed very red, a rich dark red, worn long, and confined at the nape of his neck with a black silk ribbon. He looked somehow more formidable than he had in evening dress.

He sat down at the table and ordered cold pheasant and small beer.

He said a polite good-morning. Belinda replied shyly and then he began to eat. Belinda had often heard it said that gentlemen were averse to conversation at the breakfast table, and so she ate in steady silence. She finally looked across at him, her eyes widening slightly, for he was staring at her in a way she could not fathom. It was a hard, calculating, almost predatory stare, the distillation of a long line of aristocrats who took what they wanted.

Belinda flushed slightly and looked down at her plate.

To the marquess, Belinda had become suddenly available. Any young woman who ran off with a footman could hardly be a virgin. She was not beautiful, but that mouth of hers was definitely disturbing.

'Where is Miss Pym?' asked Belinda, feeling the silence must be broken.

'I found her exploring the barbican and demanding to see the old torture chamber. What an indefatigable lady she is.'

'Why do you keep such a thing as a torture chamber?' demanded Belinda.

'For historical interest. I do not torture anyone, I assure you. There is also the dungeon, one of the towers which is said to be haunted . . .'

'By whom?'

'By the ghost of a Miss Dalrymple, a Scotch lady, governess to the children of the second earl. It was said the second earl was too interested in the lady, and so Miss Dalrymple was found murdered in the top room of the tower. Rumour had it that the countess had stabbed her to death. Another rumour had it she had rejected the advances of his lordship's *valet de chambre*.'

'And have you seen this ghost?' asked Belinda.

'I have not the necessary sensibility to see ghosts, Miss Earle.' His eyes teased her. 'Would you like me to show you the tower?'

'Yes, my lord, and perhaps Miss Pym would like to come as well.'

'But I do not know where Miss Pym is at present,' replied the marquess, ignoring the fact that he had only to summon his servants and ask them to look for her. 'We shall go now, as you have finished your breakfast.'

Belinda nodded and rose but she felt uneasy. The marquess, although his manner towards her had not particularly changed, seemed to exude a strong air of sexuality. She glanced uneasily at his flaming hair and wondered if he had a temper to match.

Hannah Pym saw them enter the courtyard together and withdrew behind a buttress. She had no wish to intrude. The marquess appeared to be chatting amiably to Belinda. She was pleased to note that Belinda was keeping quiet and obviously not treating the marquess to any of her frank disclosures of the night before. It was as well Hannah could not hear their conversation.

'None of the rooms in the walls are used now,' the marquess was saying. 'As I explained, they are merely kept in order for historical interest. Would you like to see the torture chamber first? We have a very fine rack.'

'No, I thank you,' said Belinda with a shudder, blissfully unaware that she was the first lady who had not demanded enthusiastically to see it. 'I am not the type of lady who enjoys public hangings, nor do I get a thrill from viewing antique instruments of torture. Nor do I see medieval castles as symbols of an age of chivalry and glory, but instead relics of an age of oppression.'

The curtain walls of the castle that enclosed the castle houses had four massive towers. There was a gatehouse and barbican, chapel, dungeon and torture chamber. The castle houses where the marquess lived were set in the courtyard inside the walls, rather like the buildings of Oxford College.

The marquess led the way to the tallest of the towers. Snow was falling gently, and Belinda shivered with cold. She was wearing heelless silk slippers, considered *de rigueur* for the fashionable lady, and she could feel the damp from the snow seeping through their thin soles.

'This is Robert's Tower,' said the marquess. 'Robert, Earl of Jesper, built it with the prize money he gained at Poitiers. They were great fighters, the Jespers, and when they weren't going on Crusades, or fighting the wars of various kings, they were claiming to find infidels on the Welsh and Scotch borders and murdering them as well in the name of Christianity. There are five storeys in the tower: a dungeon, three vaulted chambers, and an upper guard chamber with a store-room underneath.'

He stood back to let Belinda mount first. Suddenly self-conscious, she dropped the skirt of her gown instead of looping it over her arm to show that one leg.

She paused on the first landing until he joined her. He pushed open the door. Belinda entered.

She found herself in a large chamber, vaulted in two bays, and lit on two sides by tall, single-light ogee windows. Two grooms were sitting by the fire and rose at their entrance.

The marquess waited patiently while Belinda looked quickly around. The remains of breakfast lay on a deal table.

Then she walked out of the room. The marquess followed her and closed the door behind them.

'I thought you said the rooms were unoccupied,' whispered Belinda.

'They are,' said the marquess, surprised. 'They are only used by the outdoor servants.'

'And are not servants people?'

'My radical Miss Earle, when I said they were no longer used, I meant by either myself or my guests.'

'You are reputed to be a recluse.'

'Not I. Merely fastidious.'

Belinda climbed up the next flight of stairs. 'Now this,' said the marquess, joining her on the landing, 'is the haunted chamber.'

He was interested to see Belinda's reaction. In an age when gothic novels were in vogue, most young ladies, on being shown the tower room, would pretend to have seen the ghost; a few took the opportunity to faint into the marriageable marquess's arms. The thing about this Miss Earle, thought the marquess, was that although she was by no means beautiful, he found her large eyes and that passionate mouth immensely attractive. And her directness was refreshing. It was not a pity she was Haymarket ware; it was a definite asset as his intentions were rapidly becoming dishonourable.

Belinda stood in the middle of the room and looked slowly around. This room was not even used by the servants. It was bleak and cold, with the wind howling mournfully in the chimney.

'Was this Miss Dalrymple's room?' asked Belinda.

The marquess nodded.

There was a small chamber off the main room, a garderobe, a medieval lavatory with a stone seat over a hole, which gave a clear view downwards of the former moat, now drained. She returned to the main room, which had a scrubbed table and two massive carved chairs.

Perhaps it had not been so grim when the unfortunate governess was in residence, thought Belinda. She would surely have had some of her own possessions about her.

'I did not think they had governesses in medieval times,' said Belinda.

The marquess shrugged. He was disappointed in Belinda's lack of reaction. 'She was not called a governess. She was merely a female of fairly good birth who was there to educate the very young children. Do you sense her presence?'

Belinda shook her head. 'I sense desolation, that is all. What a cruel time to live!'

'I sometimes think no more cruel than our own,' said the marquess. 'Look from the window.'

Belinda looked out. The snow had stopped falling. Far down below, beyond the castle walls and the fields and farms and cottages, was a crossroads. And at that crossroads stood a gibbet with three rotting bodies hanging in the wind.

She shivered. 'But that is the justice of the English courts,' she said, half to herself.

'I envy you your belief in the fairness of English justice,' he said. 'One of those hanged was a half-starved youth of sixteen. He stole a sheep. The other two are murderers, and yet he met the same fate. But we become too serious. Would you like to climb to the roof of the tower?'

Belinda replied reluctantly that she would. She felt she had been discourteous in not admiring this part of the castle enough and was trying to make up for it.

They climbed higher and higher until they came to a low door that led out on to the roof of the tower.

'Go to the right,' said the marquess. 'You will obtain a good view of the castle buildings and the gardens.'

Belinda did as she was bid. She clutched the parapet and looked down at the jumble of chimneys on the roofs of the castle buildings, at the formal gardens behind them, buried in snow. The wind rose suddenly and she drew back, stepped on a pebble and gave her sprained ankle a savage wrench.

She let out a moan of pain. The marquess caught her round the waist and supported her. 'Your ankle,' he exclaimed. 'I had forgot. I should never have let you walk for so long on it. Allow me to carry you.'

Belinda protested feebly but he lifted her up easily in his arms and made for the staircase. 'Hold tightly around my neck,' he commanded. 'The stairs are narrow.'

Her heart began to thud painfully and she found it hard to breathe. He was holding her so very tightly and the feel of the hardness of his body against hers was doing bewildering things to her senses.

The marquess reached the bottom of the staircase. It was very dark there. Before he opened the door, he looked down at her and met a wide-eyed gaze. On impulse, he bent his head and kissed her on the lips. It was the first kiss Belinda had ever received and she thought dizzily that it was wickedly delicious, rather like one's first ice cream.

And then it was over. He freed her lips and said in a husky voice in which surprise and passion were mixed, 'You enchant me.' Then he opened the door and, still holding her tightly, strode across the courtyard.

From a window overlooking the courtyard, Hannah Pym looked down on the pair in deep satisfaction.

From the window of her bedchamber farther along, Penelope Jordan also saw the marquess and Belinda and bit her lips hard to stop herself from crying out. She had been schooled from birth to learn that only the vulgar showed an excess of emotion. Ladies must never laugh out loud or show anger or passion of any sort. To produce a few affecting tears to demonstrate fashionable sensibility was in order, as was the occasional swoon. Of course, a *type* of laughter was permitted, the silvery laugh, taught by one's music teacher, which began on a high note and rippled down the scale.

As she watched, the marquess set Belinda down and indicated her ankle. Then he put an arm about her waist and helped her into the house.

Penelope let out a slow breath of relief. That clever minx had affected to be suffering badly from that sprain and had cleverly manipulated Frenton into carrying her. But the marquess surely could not favour the few charms Miss Earle had above her own. Miss Earle had unfashionably high cheek-bones as well as an unfashionably large mouth.

She rang for her lady's maid and put that servant through a gruelling hour and a half – choosing clothes, brushing her hair and trying it in different styles, seeing if rouge would improve her beauty and then deciding it would not, trying on olive-green stockings and then rejecting them in favour of pink, until at long last she was nearly satisfied with her appearance.

Penelope shivered slightly despite the warmth from the bedroom fire. She was wearing a very thin spotted muslin gown under a pelisse of black lace trimmed with narrow bands of sable. On her pomaded curls the maid finally placed one of the latest turbans, decorated with two scarlet plumes to match the scarlet spot in the muslin. Penelope carefully examined her elbows, her beautiful eyes narrowing as she thought she detected a sign of red roughness on them. She carefully applied some white lead, but the two white patches stood out, so she applied more white lead to her upper arms and drew on a thin pair of scarlet gloves that reached to just below the elbow.

Then she made her way to her parents' rooms. They were in their sitting-room, breakfasting in front of a roaring fire. Her father was dining on shrimp and old ale, his favourite breakfast, while her mother had wafers of toast and tea.

'You must make ready to accompany me down-stairs,' said Penelope, cross because both were still in their undress. 'That Earle female is like to snatch the prize from me.'

'Hardly likely,' said Sir Henry. 'She is nothing out of the common way and a man as high in the instep as Frenton would not prefer the charms of some female from the stage-coach to yourself.'

'I am persuaded she is clever and cunning. I have just seen him carrying her across the courtyard. She must have pretended to have hurt her ankle again. Rally to me! There is no time to be lost.'

Hannah made her way back to the sitting-room she shared with Belinda and found that young lady sitting in an armchair while the doctor examined her ankle. 'Another bad wrench,' said the doctor. 'I shad strap it more tightly, but you must now lie in your bed with the ankle raised on a cushion.'

'It is much better now,' pleaded Belinda. 'I shall be so very bored if I have to stay confined to my bedchamber.'

'Lord Frenton,' said the doctor, strapping Belinda's ankle, 'must be anxious for you all to recommence your journey. You should oblige your host by recovering as quickly as possible.'

Hannah noticed a shadow of disappointment fall over Belinda's expressive eyes.

She waited impatiently until the doctor had taken his leave, and then asked eagerly, 'What happened? Did you really sprain that ankle again?'

'Of course I did,' said Belinda. 'He took me to the top of the tower to look at the view and I trod on a pebble and wrenched it again. He kindly offered to carry me, nay, insisted on it.' Her eyes began to shine.

'And . . . ?' prompted Hannah.

'He . . . he . . . kissed me.'

'The deuce!' Hannah looked alarmed. 'That was very fast and forward of his lordship. Your companion is laid up and your relatives are not here to protect you. Would you like me to ask him his intentions?'

'No!' said Belinda. 'I can handle my own life, Miss Pym. He seems much taken by me and even said I enchanted him.'

'Fine words don't butter any parsnips,' said Hannah crossly. 'An experienced man of the world can say anything he likes. Hark you, Miss Earle, the servants tell me that he is as good as engaged to Miss Jordan.'

'Well, that's as may be,' said Belinda doubtfully, 'but could it not be that I have struck him all of a heap?'

'Marquesses with every female in the land after 'em don't get struck that easily,' said Hannah cynically.

'Hey, what's happened to that young lady who didn't want to marry?'

'Oh, I don't *know*,' said Belinda wretchedly. 'I wish I had never told you. Now it all seems soiled.'

'Are you in love?'

'How can I tell? I have only met the man.'

'I tell you what I will do,' said Hannah. 'I will observe his behaviour towards you and let you know whether his intentions are indecent or honourable in my opinion. Would you like that?'

'No! Well, maybe yes. But I don't have to promise to listen to you.'

'Now,' said Hannah, 'I suggest you get to bed and spend the rest of the day there and I'll get two footmen to carry you down to dinner. What else did he talk about?'

'He told me about the castle and how a room in Robert's Tower was haunted by the ghost of a governess. He offered to show me the torture chamber but I said such things did not interest me, that the days of chivalry were in fact very cruel, and he said surely this age was cruel and commanded me to observe the bodies on the gibbet.'

'How eccentric!' said Hannah. 'He cannot have been trying to endear himself to you. Besides, these modern times are very humane, no racking or crushing or gouging or pouring boiling oil on people. He must have been teasing you.'

After Hannah had left, Belinda lay looking at the bed-hangings, seeing mocking faces in the patterns made by the brocade. All her elation had gone. He had only been flirting. He could not have meant anything warmer, not with his nearly-to-be fiancée as a guest. Then, despite her troubled thoughts, Belinda fell asleep.

Hannah visited the Judds in their quarters. She could see Mrs Judd had been crying. Hannah's temper snapped and she rounded on Mr Judd. 'Will you never be done with tormenting your wife?' she exclaimed. Mr Judd's face turned dark with anger and he took a menacing step towards Hannah. 'Just you try it,' said Hannah. 'I have strong arms and strong muscles, and besides that, if you lay one finger on me, I am like to brain you with the poker. Fie, for shame, you monster! Ruining your future career. One would think you had no interest in money.'

'Money!' The angry colour slowly died out of Mr Judd's face.

'Money,' echoed Mrs Judd in a whisper.

For money had been the cause of this latest marital row. Mr Judd had said his wife had cut a shabby figure at the marquess's supper table compared to the other ladies, and she had shouted at him that they had no money at all for finery and how could he be such a half-witted baboon? Aghast at his wife's temerity, Mr Judd had had no inclination to hit her, but then she had begun to cringe and cry and beg his pardon, and so he had struck her and immediately felt so guilty that he was sure his guilt must be her fault, and so he had struck her again.

'Sit down, both of you,' said Hannah, 'and listen to me. Your vanity, Mr Judd, does not seem to stretch to your playing and singing. Nor do you seem aware that your wife has a first-rate voice.'

'What has all this to do with anything?' demanded Mr Judd, his temper rising again, although he did sit down and eyed Hannah warily as if facing a dog liable to bite.

'I could not help noticing how entranced the marquess was with your singing. A couple such as you, I have heard, can command a great deal of money for a drawing-room performance, provided that couple has a patron. If you play your cards aright, you could perhaps have the marquess as that patron.'

Mr Judd looked at her open-mouthed and Mrs Judd in dawning hope.

'What is your history?' asked Hannah. 'I am not being impertinent. I only want to help.'

'It is a dreary story,' said Mr Judd. 'My father was a successful lawyer and I had a comfortable upbringing. I studied music and singing for my own pleasure. Then I met Persephone.'

What an exotic name for the frightened Mrs Judd to have, thought Hannah.

'I am from The Bath. Persephone was music teacher at the seminary where I now teach. My father disapproved of my interest in her. He had high hopes for me and wished me to enter the law. Persephone's parents had no money at all. Nonetheless, I was in love and I married her and my father turned me out.'

'And your mother?'

Mr Judd looked surprised. 'Women have no say in such matters,' he said. 'In any case, the seminary promised to engage us both, but after we had both been there for a week, they said they could not afford the two of us and so they told my wife to leave. My father and mother died a year later, both of the fever, and he had cut me out of his will. Persephone's parents are also dead. And so we struggled on. We had been to London to see if we could both find employ in different educational establishments, but we met with failure.'

Hannah turned to Mrs Judd. 'And you, where did you learn to sing so beautifully?'

'My father was a dancing master,' said Mrs Judd, 'but he had ambitions to make me an opera singer and to that end he hired the best tutors he could afford. Oh, Miss Pym, do you really think we could find a patron?'

'There is hope,' said Hannah, 'and I will have a word with his lordship myself when the time is right. But there is one thing you must do or I cannot help you.'

'That being?' demanded Mr Judd.

'No one is going to be interested in furthering the career of a constantly quarrelling couple. You must appear at all times affectionate. You must start practising in private. A woman must obey her husband, everyone knows that, but all dislike a bully, Mr Judd, and forgive me, but that is how you appear, and an unpleasant one at that.' She raised her hand to stall an angry retort from Mr Judd.

'Come now, you are not going to protest that you don't bully your wife when I and everyone else must know that you do.'

82

'He is really very kind,' said Mrs Judd, flying to her husband's defence.

'Then let him show that side of his character or I cannot help you,' said Hannah roundly.

There was a long silence after Hannah had left.

'Strange woman,' said Mr Judd gruffly.

Mrs Judd clasped her hands tightly. 'Do you think she meant what she said?'

'Yes, I do,' he said slowly. Then he gave an awkward laugh. 'I don't really *bully* you, do I, my sweet?'

The usual meek denial trembled on Mrs Judd's lips. Then she thought about the money they could make instead of scrimping and saving and rowing on the pittance paid to her husband by the seminary.

'Yes, you do, Mr Judd,' she said firmly. 'You are become a monster. You nag and criticize me for every little fault and my life is wretched.'

Mr Judd looked uneasily round as if expecting to find the marquess or Hannah Pym listening.

To apologize for or to admit to his bad behaviour would be going too far. And yet there was a steely determination in his little wife's eyes that had not been there before.

'And if you do anything to jeopardize our future by indulging your bad temper,' said Mrs Judd, 'I shall *leave* you.'

He looked as startled as if some mild-mannered family pet had suddenly decided to savage him. 'We'll see how it goes,' he mumbled, and Mrs Judd, knowing her husband well, realized that was as near an apology and a promise of reform as she was likely to get.

Hannah went into Miss Wimple's bedchamber and was reassured to see that lady looking much recovered.

'How is Belinda?' demanded Miss Wimple in stern accents.

'Very well,' said Hannah. Her eyes sharpened. 'Have you had a visit from his lordship?'

Miss Wimple put a hand to her brow. 'I recall he came to see me last night.'

'And what did you say?'

Miss Wimple bridled. 'I do not see that what I said or did not say is any of your concern, Miss Pym.'

'But Miss Earle should be your concern, Miss Wimple. That, after all, is what you are being paid for. You did not, by any chance, let fall to his lordship about Miss Earle's unfortunate episode with the footman?'

'I cannot remember what I said,' said Miss Wimple huffily. 'My head aches. Go away.'

'I wish to counsel you to hold your tongue on that matter in future,' said Hannah, 'for the young lady may arrive in Bath with a reputation already ruined and, if that be the case, I shall have no hesitation in telling her parents the reason for her downfall. If you did let fall anything indiscreet about your charge, then I suggest you tell his lordship as soon as possible that you were rambling.'

Miss Wimple lay very still after Hannah had left. She did recall what she had said to the marquess. She had felt it her duty, thought Miss Wimple defiantly, not knowing that she had been prompted by the jealousy of an unmarried middle-aged woman of small means for a young lady of fortune. She would not eat her words when she saw the marquess, but mindful of her job and Miss Pym's threat, she would beg him to keep silent on the matter.

And so it came about that Miss Wimple did more damage to Belinda's reputation than she had done before. She sent for the marquess and begged him so emotionally never to speak of Belinda's affair with the footman that she left him thinking that Miss Earle must have behaved very shockingly indeed.

Dinner was served at four in the afternoon, so at three-thirty all were assembled in the Cedar Room, Belinda having been carried in by two footmen.

With the single-mindedness of the aristocrat, the marquess studied Belinda Earle quite openly, unaware of the consternation he was causing in the Jordan family. She attracted him and he still remembered that kiss vividly and wanted more. But to seduce, say, a London widow who knew very well what she was about was one thing. To go to the bedchamber of a gently reared girl whom her family was obviously trying to reform was another. In some way, Belinda must show him she knew what she was doing and was prepared to face the consequences.

Hannah saw that studied look and her heart fell. There was something more of the predator about it than the lover. Her mind went back to a certain groom who had worked for Mr Clarence. Hannah had been courted and then rejected by a perfidious under-butler and had been left feeling raw and stupid. The groom, Harry Bates, was rumoured to be the bastard son of a noble. He had a certain aristocratic elegance, strange in a groom, and more intelligence than was usual. He was witty and made Hannah laugh at a time when she did not feel like laughing at anything. It was well known among the staff at Thornton Hall that Hannah rose very early before the rest to spend a little time by herself in the servants' hall. It was there Harry had approached her one morning. She had been delighted to see him, but he had sat down very close to her at the table, and then he had taken her hand and gazed into her eyes. In his eyes, Hannah had seen the same look that the marquess had in his when he studied Belinda – that authoritative air of reaching out and taking what he wanted. And all in that moment, Hannah had realized that Harry thought she had had an affair with the under-butler and so was fair game.

She had snatched her hand away, and with her face flaming had said, 'I am still a virgin,' and had walked out of the servants' hall. Harry had never come near her again.

In her heart, she cursed Miss Wimple. She was sure the companion had gossiped about Belinda. The Jordans, she noticed, were looking furious. Little did they know they had nothing to be furious about, thought Hannah gloomily.

And Belinda! A pox on the girl! Hannah felt quite

savage. Belinda was glowing and her looks had taken on a radiance.

'I hear Miss Wimple is all but recovered,' said Penelope in a thin voice. 'You will soon be able to take your leave.'

'Not in this weather,' said Hannah.

'But the weather has changed,' said Sir Henry with satisfaction. 'Listen!'

They all listened, and sure enough, instead of snow whispering at the windows, they heard the sound of drumming rain.

'The roads will be flooded for days,' Hannah pointed out.

'But not as far as the nearest inn, where no doubt your stage is waiting,' put in Lady Jordan.

'Come now,' chided the marquess, 'you must not be in such a hurry to speed our guests on their way. I, for one, am hoping that Mr and Mrs Judd will entertain us again this evening.'

'Gladly,' said the Judds in chorus.

Dinner was announced and the guests filed through to the dining-room. Once more, Belinda was seated beside the marquess.

'I am amazed, Miss Earle,' said the marquess, almost as soon as they were seated, 'that you were not besieged with suitors during your Season.'

'I do not remember you at the Season,' said Penelope, forgetting her manners in her anger and talking directly across the table.

'I was mostly hidden from view,' said Belinda with a gurgle of laughter. 'I used to take a book with me and try to hide behind a potted plant to while away the tedium of the evening.'

'Penelope,' said Sir Henry heavily, 'was never without partners.'

The marquess frowned. He could hardly be so rude as to remind them of the conventions and urge them to talk only to the people on either side. The unsophisticated Judds had taken a leaf out of the Jordans' book and were talking openly to all at the table, inoffensive chit-chat about the weather and the perils of the English roads.

Penelope saw her advantage and took it. She began to talk directly to the marquess about people they both knew, leaving Belinda and Hannah excluded.

Belinda had never been jealous in her life, but now she was shaken to the very core of her being. She hated Penelope Jordan. He had kissed *her*, not Penelope, and he had said she enchanted him. Belinda craved some sign from him that he cared for her. Her strict upbringing was being undermined with jealousy and all her usual common sense had fled. This was agony! She would ask to see him alone and, yes, she would ask him if he loved her.

Things were worse when they retired to the Cedar Room. The Judds gave a virtuoso performance, each liquid note of their voices tearing at Belinda's heart. Mrs Judd was so very happy and it showed in her singing. It was obvious to Hannah that the Judds had taken her advice, but she was so worried about Belinda that it gave her little satisfaction.

Belinda had fallen helplessly in love, and she did

not know what to do. The marquess looked so very handsome, but unapproachable. His hair was powdered and he was dressed in fine silk and the jewels in his cravat and at his fingers winked and blazed in the candle-light. His eyes gave nothing away. He seemed totally wrapped up in the music, as indeed he was.

Hannah edged her chair closer to that of the marquess and when the Judds had finished one number and were looking through their music, she said softly, 'It is a pity two such fine singers should languish forgotten. They need a patron.'

'Meaning I should sponsor them,' he said, looking amused.

'Why not?'

'Why not, indeed, Miss Pym. I shall speak to them about it.'

'Oh, thank you,' said Hannah. 'Did . . . did Miss Wimple mention anything to you about Miss Earle?'

'Such as?' His eyes were quite blank.

'I feel Miss Wimple is not a suitable companion for Miss Earle,' said Hannah. 'She . . .'

But he held up his hand for silence, for the Judds had begun to sing again.

Belinda decided she would write him a note, asking him to meet her. She would do it as soon as she retired and give the note to one of the servants. But Miss Pym must not know.

At last the evening was over. The marquess suggested Belinda might like to retire to rest her injured ankle and his glance included the other stage-coach passengers. He was sitting beside Penelope, engrossed in conversation, when Belinda and Hannah left the room. Belinda hobbled and leaned on Hannah's arm, for she felt being carried by footmen presented too undignified a spectacle. She twisted her head and looked back. Penelope was smiling at something the marquess was saying and leaning towards him, creating an island of intimacy, while her parents beamed on the pair as if already blessing the newly-weds.

After Belinda had said good night to Hannah, she went to her room. She dismissed the maid, saying she would prepare herself for bed. Instead, she sat down at a tiny escritoire in the corner and wrote a short note, asking the Marquess of Frenton to exchange a few words with her before he retired for the night. She sanded the letter and sealed it. She reached out a hand to the bell-rope and then paused. Miss Pym might hear the sound of the bell and come to see if anything was wrong.

She gently opened her bedroom door and walked along the corridor. A small boy was trimming one of the lamps that stood in an embrasure. Belinda handed him the letter and told him to take it to the marquess and then returned to her room, feeling very alone and frightened and wondering if she had run mad.

The lamp-boy was too inferior a being to convey a message to the marquess directly. He gave it to the fourth footman, who took it down to the servants' hall and gave it to the butler in front of everyone, saying it was from Miss Earle to the marquess. The butler put on his coat, put the letter on a silver tray, and carried it upstairs.

The Jordans were in the Cedar Room and on the point of saying their good-nights to the marquess. The butler handed him the letter, but, being a good servant and scenting an intrigue, he did not say who had sent it.

The marquess turned away slightly and scanned the short note. His lips curled in a smile.

Penelope Jordan found out who had sent that letter as her maid prepared her for bed. All the servants knew. So she, too, wrote a letter and sent her maid with it to Hannah Pym.

'As you are obviously concerned for the welfare of your fellow passenger,' she wrote, 'I suggest you stop Miss Earle writing letters to the Marquess of Frenton proposing assignations.' Penelope of course did not know what Belinda's letter had said but felt sure that as Belinda had written something she could obviously not say in public, that meant an assignation. 'I beg you to tell the silly child that I am engaged to Frenton and any attempts on her part to secure his affections would only lead to ridicule.'

5

Belinda looked at the little gilt clock on the mantel which was flanked by a shepherd and shepherdess. Midnight!

Surely he would come.

She bit her lip remembering the conversation she had had with Hannah Pym before that lady retired for the night. Miss Pym had said roundly that the marquess's intentions were definitely dishonourable, doubly so as he had kissed Belinda while courting another. Belinda had only pretended to listen, as she had in the past when someone was giving her a jaw-me-dead.

But Hannah's words echoed in her brain. If he was an honourable man, then he should have called on her immediately after reading her note. If he was dishonourable, then he would wait until he was sure everyone was asleep and then call on her. That could not be the case. He must be waiting until morning.

She gave a disappointed little sigh. Slowly she removed her clothes and washed herself and pulled on a lacy night-gown and tied her nightcap on her head. She climbed into bed and blew out the candle on the bedside table. She studied the patterns made by the flickering flames from the fire on the walls. Then she realized the rain had ceased to fall. She climbed down from the bed again and drew the curtains and looked out. A full moon was shining and the courtyard glinted with puddles of melting snow. She tugged open the window and leaned out. The air was soft and spring-like. Her days at the castle were numbered. She had looked in on Miss Wimple with Hannah before they retired to their rooms and Belinda had been astonished at how quickly her companion was recovering her health.

She limped back to the bed, sadly climbed back in, and drew the blankets up to her chin.

There came a soft knock at the door and her heart began to thud. Servants never knocked. She got out of bed and went to open it.

The Marquess of Frenton walked straight past her and stood in the middle of the room. He smiled at her and opened his arms. Belinda closed the door and then turned and ran straight into them. Faint warning bells were ringing at the back of her mind; he was wearing a night-gown and dressing-gown and she herself was in her undress. But as his lips closed down over her own in a passionate kiss she forgot time and space and everything but the hot surgings of her own body pressed so tightly against his. Her fingers wound themselves in his long red hair still faintly scented from the hair powder that he had brushed out, and she moaned against his lips.

Hannah Pym awoke and was immediately uneasy. The first thing she thought of was that Belinda Earle had accepted her strictures too easily. She was sure that young lady was planning mischief. She was thirsty and decided to get herself a glass of water. She lit the bed-candle and then rose and went to the toilet table, which held a decanter of drinking water. Then she saw a note that had been pushed under the door. When Penelope's maid had come to deliver it, she had scratched at the door and, receiving no answer, decided Miss Pym was asleep.

Hannah opened it and read it. Then she cocked her head to one side and pulled her nose in embarrassed distress. She was sure there were faint sounds coming from Belinda's bedchamber.

Hannah lifted the candle and walked with a determined step through the sitting-room and straight into Belinda's bedchamber.

Belinda was clasped in the marquess's arms. They did not hear her come in. Both were apparently deaf to the world.

'Stop that!' said Hannah. 'Stop it this minute, I say!'

The couple fell apart. Belinda was flushed and aghast, the marquess angry.

'What do you want, Miss Pym?' he demanded in a cold, thin voice.

'What do I want?' echoed Hannah. 'The question, my lord, is what do you want?'

'A word with you in private, Miss Pym,' he said grimly.

Hannah led the way into the little sitting-room and closed the door firmly on Belinda.

'My lord,' said Hannah, 'I do not wish to abuse your hospitality by interfering with your pleasures. But Miss Earle is no woman of the world. Nay, sir, neither is she a woman of the streets. It is well known in this household that you are courting Miss Jordan. I must ask you what your intentions are towards Miss Earle.'

'And may I point out,' he said calmly, 'that my intentions are none of your business.'

'Someone must make it their business,' exclaimed Hannah. 'You cannot seduce a virgin and expect me to stand by and see it happen.'

'It is my understanding that Miss Earle is not a virgin, and she certainly does not behave like one. I was in her bedchamber at her invitation.'

'You silly . . . lord, she thinks you love her. Has Miss Wimple been filling your ears with some tale about a footman?'

'Yes.'

'Then I feel it my duty to tell you exactly what happened.'

And Hannah did.

The marquess stood frowning as she talked. There was no doubting the honesty of the story Miss Pym told. He began to wonder what on earth he would have done had he stayed in Belinda's arms much longer. He might have seduced a highly respectable lady.

But he was a gentleman, and gentlemen never apologize because everyone knows gentlemen never make mistakes.

'I was misled,' he said. 'But I think it would be too mortifying to explain to Miss Earle that I thought she was a hussy. Pray tell her I was foxed.'

'I will try,' said Hannah doubtfully, 'but you look cold-stone sober.'

'Tell her anything you like. I note the weather is improving. My servants tell me that your stage is repaired and waiting at the Queen Bess in Comfrey. We will give Miss Wimple another day's rest and then convey you all there. Whether Miss Wimple feels up to travelling on further from the inn will be a matter for her to decide.'

'It is a pity,' mourned Hannah. 'You are both so well suited.'

'Miss Jordan and I?'

'No, my lord, you and Miss Earle.'

He looked on her in dawning amusement. She was an odd creature with her strangely coloured eyes and her thin spare body and crooked nose. 'Marriage is a serious business, Miss Pym. I fear you have been reading romances. I will choose some lady who will grace my home.'

'Like an art treasure?'

'Miss Pym, has anyone ever told you that you get away with murder? I really do not know why I am standing here listening to your strictures. Pray tell Miss Earle I behaved badly and am ashamed of myself.'

'Why not tell her yourself?'

Why not? The marquess paused. He had never shirked an unpleasant duty in his life before. But the effect Belinda Earle had on his senses was devastating.

'To be brutally frank, Miss Pym, I do not trust myself alone in a bedchamber with Miss Earle.'

'Ah!' Hannah's eyes gleamed with a gold light. She decided to say no more at present. With any luck, this marquess was in love with Belinda and did not know it.

'Then if you will leave this way, my lord,' said Hannah. She showed him through her bedchamber to the corridor door, ushered him out, and then returned through the sitting-room to Belinda's bedchamber.

Belinda was sitting by the fire. She had lit an oil-lamp and her eyes were bleak as she looked at Hannah. 'How dare you!' said Belinda.

Hannah silently handed her the letter from Penelope Jordan. Belinda read it and her face went as red as the fire she was sitting beside.

'Yes, all the servants must know. To whom did you give your letter?'

'To a lamp-boy,' said Belinda.

'A humble lamp-boy is of too low a rank to carry a letter to a marquess. You should have known that. Do your aunt and uncle not have many servants?'

Belinda shook her head. 'No, we only have a butler, two footmen, two housemaids, two chambermaids, a lady's maid, a cook, a housekeeper, one kitchen maid, one odd man, and of course the coachman and groom.'

'Then I must tell you that the lamp-boy would take that letter of yours to the servants' hall, where it would be delivered to the butler. The lamp-boy would tell the butler in front of the others from whom it came. So it would no doubt get to the ears of Miss Jordan's lady's maid and so to me.'

Belinda's anger had died. The full horror of what she had done was slowly dawning on her. Love had blinded her to the fact that the Marquess of Frenton regarded her as a slut and therefore easy game. How shabby and brassy and common she now must appear set beside the beautiful Penelope.

Hannah did not want to add to Belinda's distress by telling her the marquess knew about that footman episode. Both Belinda and the marquess were ashamed of themselves. Good! If the passage of true love ran smooth, then it could not possibly end happily, in Hannah's experience. She remembered a gamekeeper at Thornton Hall who had fallen in love with a pretty chambermaid, and she with him. Mrs Clarence was still in residence and had smiled on the lovers. Everyone had thought they were a perfect match and said so. Before the gamekeeper had even thought of popping the question, Mrs Clarence had called him in and offered him a cottage on the estate where he could live with his bride. The couple had grown shy and embarrassed and awkward at all this headlong enthusiasm to get them to the altar, and love had faded away. Such a pity, thought Hannah. Their characters had been so well matched. She always thought that had a few obstacles been thrown in their way, then they might have tied the knot and lived happily ever after because they were so compatible, and couples must have something other than love between them to survive the rocky road of marriage.

'I suppose I should be grateful to you for interrupting us when you did,' said Belinda awkwardly.

'It was very painful for me,' said Hannah. 'In future, Miss Earle, no matter how strong your feelings, you must let the men do the pursuing. That is the way of the world. Any bold move on the female's part is always misinterpreted, and men only value what is hard to get. The weather is improving, and we shall shortly be moving on.'

'I would rather leave on the morrow,' said Belinda in a low voice.

'Too soon,' said Hannah. 'One more day. Take my advice and keep to your bedchamber and do not venture belowstairs. Or sit and read to Miss Wimple. She needs her mind improved. The marquess will at first be relieved at your absence and then he will miss you.'

'I do not want him to miss me,' said Belinda pettishly. 'The least he could do is apologize.'

'You can hardly expect him to do that after having sent that letter and given him the wrong impression.'

'Am I so very bad, Miss Pym? Am I going to be damned as an Original? Why cannot I behave as other young misses?' Tears stood out in Belinda's eyes.

'Not your fault,' said Hannah gruffly. 'If that uncle and aunt were here, I would wring their necks. This is the direct result of overmuch discipline and reaching too high in the Marriage Market. Had they left you alone, you might have waited until your inheritance and found someone suitable without a title.'

'It is dangerous to live on dreams,' said Belinda with a little sigh. 'I thought I was in love, but perhaps it was only because I am dreading the thought of Great-Aunt Harriet and months and months of moralizing. It would have been a triumph to arrive on her fusty doorstep already engaged to a marquess. Heigh-ho! I am feeling much chastened, Miss Pym, but better in spirit. I shall survive.'

The marquess, next day reviewing the events of the night, began to wonder if he *had* been drunk. He convinced himself that the repairs begun on the roof of a tenant's cottage at one of the farther corners of his estate needed personal attention. Then he decided to ride on to the Queen Bess in Comfrey. There he met the new driver of the stage-coach, who told him that the young driver and the guard who had caused the accident had been fired. The landlord assured his lordship that rooms would be available for the stage-coach passengers when they arrived. The road from the castle to the Queen Bess was clear. They would need, however, to stay at the inn for about two days, as the roads farther on were flooded. The marquess paid the innkeeper for their care and accommodation. Satisfied, he rode back to the castle. The stage-coach passengers could leave the next morning. Miss Wimple would be conveyed lying down in a separate carriage. She would be put to bed at the inn, and from then on she would no longer be the marquess's responsibility.

He dressed carefully for dinner that afternoon, as if armouring himself in silk and jewels for the confrontation with Belinda. But when he descended to the Cedar Room, he was told by Miss Pym that Belinda's ankle was still hurting and she preferred to take her meals in her sitting-room and to read to Miss Wimple.

The marquess was at first relieved, and then, as dinner progressed, disappointed. The day had turned flat. He looked at Penelope Jordan and imagined sitting with her at dinner-tables and supper-tables day in and day out, and suddenly realized it was a prospect he could not face.

After dinner Mr Judd, trembling with nerves, took the marquess aside and asked him if he could really be of any help in finding them singing engagements. The marquess, glad he could do something so simple, agreed and wrote the Judds letters of introduction to all the leading luminaries of Bath, including the Master of Ceremonies at the Pump Room.

The Judds, overwhelmed with relief and delight, sang like angels. Far above the Cedar Room, in Miss Wimple's bedchamber, Belinda heard the music. She could picture the marquess sitting beside Penelope, the perfect couple.

She dropped the book she had been reading in her lap and said to her companion, 'Did you by any chance, Miss Wimple, take it upon yourself to warn his lordship about my adventure with the footman?'

'I did tell him,' said Miss Wimple, 'but I was overset at the time. Therefore, I sent for him yesterday and swore him to silence. I did my duty.'

Belinda controlled her rage and mortification with an effort. 'Do you never think to your future, Miss Wimple?' she asked. 'In two years' time, I will reach my majority and become an independent lady of means, a lady of means who will not want to be saddled with a companion who acts like a self-righteous jailer.'

Outraged, Miss Wimple sat up in bed. 'Wait until I tell your aunt and uncle what you have said.'

'Tell them,' said Belinda bitterly. 'What more can they do to me? Read to yourself, Miss Wimple. In case you have not been paying attention, it is a book of Mr Porteous's sermons. Perhaps it might improve the low tenor of your mind.'

When Belinda left, Miss Wimple lay thinking uneasily. She enjoyed the power her position as a sort of wardress to Belinda Earle had given her. She had no intention of stooping so low as to ingratiate herself with that young minx. As soon as they reached Bath, she would search around for a suitable post, and to revenge herself further on Belinda, she would do as much damage to that young lady's reputation as she possibly could. It was an unfair world where a young lady of low morals such as Belinda Earle should be blessed with a fortune when such as she, of high moral standing, should be forced to work for a living.

The morning dawned fine and sparkling and sunny. A fresh warm wind blew across the countryside and blackbirds were singing from the battlements as the stage-coach passengers made their way to the court-yard. Mrs Judd was bubbling over with high spirits. Not only had her husband been treating her affection-ately, even in private, but the marquess had given them a handsome sum in gold to enable them to start on their new career. She planned gown after gown, visions of silks and muslins and cambrics and velvets floating through her happy brain. She did not realize that the bullying had ceased not only because of her husband's ambitions, but because her own attitude had changed. She no longer crept or cringed or punctuated his every pontification with 'Yes, dear.'

The marquess was not present. The butler told them his lordship had been called away to attend to an urgent matter on the estates. Heavy of heart, Belinda climbed into the carriage. She looked up at the mullioned windows of the castle houses flashing in the sun, and as she did so one of the windows swung open and Penelope Jordan leaned out.

She saw Belinda looking up and gave a mocking wave and her beautiful lips curled in a slow smile. Belinda stuck out her tongue and then jerked down the carriage blind and sat with her arms folded.

The marquess, on horseback, was on a hill that

looked down on the Bath road and watched the carriages roll out through the lodge-gates, the first carriage bearing Belinda and Miss Pym, the second the Judds, and the third, Miss Wimple. He restrained a sudden impulse to ride down and join the carriages and accompany them to the inn. He was well shot of Belinda Earle. But he could still feel her lips against his own, warm and eager and, yes, he finally had to admit it, totally innocent.

Back at the castle, the Jordans were waiting for him. He sighed. High time he got rid of them as well and returned to his comfortable days of isolation. He would tell them he had to travel somewhere or another and soften the blow by saying they were welcome to stay, sure that once their quarry had flown, they would not do so.

That evening, he was doomed to disappointment. The Jordans were rich and remained rich by guarding every penny apart from what they spent on Penelope's extravagant gowns and jewels. Sir Henry jovially said they would be only too happy to await Frenton's return. The marquess parried by saying he might be gone for some considerable time. Lady Henry smiled gently and remarked coyly that their dear Penelope would act as chatelaine in his absence. 'Good practice, hey?' said Sir Henry and again gave that false jovial laugh that was beginning to grate on the marquess's ears.

Now he would have to find somewhere to go. But where? London out of Season was not to his taste.

The Queen Bess was an impressive Elizabethan inn with three lofty storeys forming bay windows supported by brackets and caryatids. Inside, it was panelled in wainscot with carved ceilings adorned with dolphins, cherubim and acorns bordered with wreaths of flowers. The sign over the door was excellently painted, probably because Queen Elizabeth was always generally well treated in both busts and portraits, for such as were executed by unskilful artists were by her own order 'knocked in pieces and cast into the fire'. A proclamation of 1563 recites that:

Her Majestie perceiveth that a great number of Hir loving subjects are much greved and take great offence with the errors and deformities alredy committed by sondry persons in this behalf, she straightly chargeth all her officers and ministers to see to the observation hereof, and as soon as may be, to reform the error alredy committed, and in the mean tyme to forbydd and prohibit the showing of such as are apparently deformed until they may be reformed that are reformable.

Queen Elizabeth was, of course, supposed to have slept there, although Hannah thought that, with a castle so near at hand, it was unlikely she would opt for a bed in a common inn. The room that Belinda shared with Hannah, having refused to share a bedchamber with Miss Wimple, was said to be haunted by the ghost of a grey lady. The landlord said this was an added attraction. Hannah, suspecting an addition to the bill for the pleasures of sharing a room with a ghost, demanded the price and was surprised and delighted when the landlord told her that the Marquess of Frenton had already paid handsomely for the stage-coach passengers' food and lodging.

As they hung their clothes away in the wardrobe, Hannah said cheerfully to Belinda that she was sure their one great adventure was all they would have on this journey, the Bath road being famous for its safety and absence of footpads and highwaymen. Belinda's face fell. Although she did not exactly wish Miss Wimple's death, she could not help hoping another accident would befall that lady. Coping with Great-Aunt Harriet was something she felt she might be able to do herself were not Miss Wimple around to drop poison into that relative's ear.

They were to take up another passenger when they resumed their journey, a Methodist minister called Mr Biles, who was residing at the inn. Hannah thought, when they all met up at the dinner-table, that he looked surprisingly like Miss Wimple. He had the same heavy features and the same moralizing manner, and the same weakness for strong drink. Hannah told him of their adventures, to which he replied that God moved in mysterious ways. Hannah described the accident to Miss Wimple. Mr Biles said solemnly that his duty lay with the patient and he would call on her. Hannah enthusiastically agreed, adding she was sure Miss Wimple would find a strong sermon very fortifying, and did Mr Biles have one with him? Mr

Biles replied that he prided himself on giving extempore sermons, to which Hannah retorted, 'All the better.' After dinner, she cheerfully led him to Miss Wimple's bedchamber and shut the door on the couple, considering that a middle-aged spinster and a minister need not worry about the conventions.

'But,' mocked a voice in her head, 'say you yourself were alone with Sir George Clarence in an inn bedchamber . . .'

Her mind clamped down on the thought. Sir George, brother of her late employer, had befriended her, it was true. But he was far above her. To think of him in any terms warmer than admiration and friendship was folly and impertinence.

She went back downstairs. The Judds and Belinda had moved to the coffee room.

'I do not like Miss Wimple,' said Belinda in a low voice, 'but do you not think Mr Biles too strong a punishment for anyone?'

'No, I think they will deal together extremely well.'

But when Mr Biles eventually reappeared, Hannah wondered if she had done the right thing. There was a definite reforming gleam in his eye as he surveyed Belinda. Hannah privately damned Miss Wimple as a malicious gossip and took herself upstairs to remind that lady that if she told anyone at all about Belinda's unfortunate experience, she, Hannah Pym, would have no alternative but to report her to her employers.

Not knowing that Hannah had only guessed that she had been talking about Belinda, Miss Wimple thought it was Mr Biles who had told her and felt mortified, for had she not sworn the minister to secrecy? But Mr Biles called on her before bedtime and protested his innocence with such vehemence that Miss Wimple's spirits were restored. And then, to add fuel to her malice towards her charge, a letter for her arrived by hand from the castle. It was from Penelope Jordan, who wrote that Belinda had been flirting shamelessly with the marquess and had even written to him arranging an assignation. She begged Miss Wimple to be careful of her charge, saying she had warned Miss Pym about the proposed assignation as she felt poor Miss Wimple was too ill to cope, but it was obvious that Miss Pym had lax morals and had done nothing.

With a sigh of satisfaction, Miss Wimple showed Mr Biles the letter.

After exclaiming in horror at the contents, Mr Biles asked who this Miss Jordan was.

'She is a young lady of sterling character,' said Miss Wimple, concealing the fact that, because of her accident, she had not set eyes on her. 'The house-keeper who was nursing me told me she is to wed the Marquess of Frenton. What am I to do with that wretched girl? First a footman, and now she is wantonly pursuing a marquess who has no intention of marrying her.'

'I shall speak to her and bring her to recognize the folly of her ways,' said Mr Biles, who was enjoying all this intrigue immensely. But Miss Wimple thought of Hannah Pym and shuddered. She did not want to lose her comfortable and well-paid position as companion to Belinda until she had secured another post. 'It would not serve,' she said firmly. 'We both travel to The Bath. May I persuade you to assist me in keeping an eye on the young lady?'

'It is my duty as a man of the cloth,' he said sententiously. 'No man shall come near her when I am nigh.'

'He was back in her bedchamber again,' said Hannah as she and Belinda prepared for bed, 'and I fear she is a gossip. I am perfectly sure she told him about that footman.'

'She must be stopped!' said Belinda, aghast.

'Yes, but how?' Hannah sat down on the edge of the bed next to Belinda and, worried though she was, studied her feet, of which she was inordinately proud, with some complacency. 'I fear I shall have to call on your aunt when we reach Bath and explain to her that your companion is ruining your reputation.'

'I suppose I should not refine on it too much.' Belinda sighed. 'It is not as if a Methodist minister is the height of fashion. He will not frequent the same circles as Great-Aunt Harriet.'

'But the Marquess of Frenton will,' said Hannah.

Shocked and dismayed, Belinda stared at her. 'Yes, my dear,' said Hannah. 'Now that we are away from the castle, I must tell you that Miss Wimple must have told Frenton about that footman, and in such terms that he thought you open to his advances.'

Belinda hung her head. 'How *mortifying.* Miss Wimple did tell me. But I was silly enough to think he might have cared for me a little. Who am I, after all, when compared to such as Penelope Jordan?'

'You are a young lady of heart and feeling,' said Hannah. 'It was the marquess who came out of that adventure badly and not you. Now that he knows you to be respectable, for you may be sure I put him straight on that matter, he may readjust his thoughts. The Jordans are dull, and despite lineage and money, very common. If he cares for you at all, he will come and find you. If all he wanted was an easy diversion, then you are much better off without him.'

'It makes him seem so much less noble,' said Belinda. 'I thought he was so far above me. He behaved disgracefully, for even had I lost my honour to that footman, I am still an unmarried young lady of good family and not some tavern wench.'

'That kind never stops to think when something they want comes across their path.' Hannah patted Belinda's hand. 'I heard a little from the servants. He was left quite poor when his father died and restored the family fortune by intelligence and hard work. But a marquess is a marquess, and money or not, he must have been courted and fêted as soon as he was out of short coats. Any female he wants is his for the taking. Do you still care for him?'

Belinda shook her head in bewilderment. 'I cannot think clearly. Every time I try to think of him, I can only think of my own wanton behaviour. Passion is a cheat, as you surely know, Miss Pym.'

Hannah looked at Belinda doubtfully. Ladies did not feel passion. Everyone knew that, or rather, everyone except Belinda Earle. She herself had never been swayed by such feelings, even when she was the lowest of servants. Certainly, she had been smitten by that under-butler, but that had been a shy and tremulous yearning of the spirit for a friend. Men had lusts, women had love, that was the difference. Perhaps Belinda's ancestors had slipped up somewhere and introduced a vulgar strain into the blood.

'Was Miss Wimple very angry when you said you would not share a room with her?' asked Hannah, changing the subject as they both climbed into bed.

'Not really. I told her that, as an invalid, she would be better in a room by herself. Are not the conventions strange, Miss Pym? For all we know, Miss Wimple may have been indulging in Roman orgies with Mr Biles, and yet it is all right for them to be locked up in a bedchamber together.'

Hannah began to giggle helplessly. 'Why, what is the matter?' asked Belinda.

'I am trying *not* to imagine Miss Wimple indulging in orgies,' laughed Hannah. 'Did you mark her head? Her hair has started to grow in, a sort of fuzz all over. She looks like a fledgling vulture.'

'Have you ever seen a vulture?' asked Belinda, settling back against the pillows and hoping to wheedle a bedtime story from her new friend.

'I saw a drawing in a book in the library in Thornton Hall.'

'Did you always read much?'

'No,' said Hannah. 'I was barely literate when I arrived at Thornton Hall, but so ambitious!'

'So how did you learn to read and write? Oh, I know. I wager it was the beautiful Mrs Clarence.'

'Yes. It was when I was the between-stairs maid. She found me one day glaring at a newspaper and turning it this way and that, and asked me gently if I could read. I said I could only make out a very few of the words. But she had hired a nursery maid—'

'She had children? You did not mention children.'

Hannah shook her head sadly. 'She was so very sure she would have children, don't you see. She had a nursery all prepared, cradle and toys, and everything so dainty and pretty. She hired the nursery maid, saying she had such a good reputation she wanted to snatch her up while she could. But nothing ever happened. I remember one day passing the nursery and hearing singing. Mrs Clarence was sitting there, rocking the empty cradle and singing a lullaby. It made me cry. I never told anyone.'

Hannah fell silent.

'The nursery maid,' prompted Belinda gently.

'She was young and kind. I think she came from quite a good family which had come down in the world. I was given half an hour's lesson by her each evening. Her name was Dorothy Friend, and she was a Quaker. A suitable name for a Quaker. I learned very rapidly. Then Mr Clarence grew impatient with what he called "this farce of a nursery" and she was dismissed. Mrs Clarence found her a post in another household. But by the time she was dismissed, I had learned to read and write and add and subtract figures. Sometimes, when I look back over my life,' said Hannah sadly, 'I do not think of all the people who harmed me, but quite often of all the kindnesses and wish I could go back and say "thank you" properly.'

She closed her eyes. But Belinda did not want to be left alone with thoughts of the marquess.

'Did you always want to travel?' she asked.

Hannah shook her head. 'For a long time, I was content, working my way up. But when Mrs Clarence ran away, half the servants were dismissed and half the house shut up. It was sad and gloomy, and without guests there was little work to do compared with what had gone before. Thornton Hall began to seem like a prison. I would rise very early each morning, make tea, and then slip up to the drawing-room and open the windows and wait for the first stage-coach to go hurtling by, far away from Thornton Hall.'

'Was Mr Clarence kind?'

'Oh, he was a good employer. I wish he had been a better husband. Sir George, his brother, told me that Mr Clarence was always a difficult and moody man and it was that which had driven his wife away.'

There was a note of pride in Hannah's voice when she mentioned Sir George.

'This Sir George Clarence, do you know him well?' asked Belinda.

'Quite well,' said Hannah. 'He was most kind after my employer died. He arranged a bank account for me and he took me to tea at Gunter's.'

'Is he married?'

'No,' said Hannah stiffly.

'But he took you to Gunter's.'

'As I said, he is most kind.'

'How old is he?'

'What questions you do ask, my child. Fifties.'

'Aha!' said Belinda.

'And what does that "aha" mean?'

'It means, Miss Pym, that a marriageable bachelor took you to Gunter's.'

'Sir George is an honourable and kind gentleman, that is all,' said Hannah, suddenly cross with Belinda, but not knowing why. 'Go to sleep!'

Belinda turned over on her side. Between a crack in the bed-hangings shone a spark of light from the rushlight on the bedside table. She stared at it, hypnotized, trying to concentrate on that pin-point of light and empty her brain of thoughts of the marquess. But the thoughts came just the same . . . What was he doing? . . . Did he think of her?

The Marquess of Frenton was being prepared for bed by his Swiss manservant. He turned over the day in his mind. Penelope had started to give orders to the servants as if she were already the lady of the castle. He had to admit he felt trapped. He had at no time expressed a wish to marry her, and yet by inviting her and her parents to the castle as his only guests, he had led her to believe he would marry her.

He must get away. But he could not bear to leave the Jordans in residence.

But where?

He had a married sister, Mary, Lady Arnold, who lived in Bath. He had not seen Mary in some time and a visit was long overdue. He was not very fond of his

114

sister, for Mary, older than he by three years, had seen no point in his determination in the early days to keep the castle and estates. She was anxious to secure a good dowry and saw the maintenance of the castle as eating up any possible dowry she might have. But she had married well, although she was fond of saying it was thanks to her own efforts and no thanks to her brother. Still, she was his sister and he should pay her a call.

He wondered about Miss Earle and what she thought of him, or if she thought of him. He should be grateful to the redoubtable Miss Pym for interrupting them. He wished now he had not been in such a hurry to be shot of the stage-coach passengers. Miss Pym had entertained him with her forthright manner and the singing of the Judds had been a delight. Belinda Earle had enjoyed the music, to which Penelope appeared totally deaf. He remembered Belinda's expressive face and the emotions flitting across her large eyes. Why was it considered bad ton for women to betray emotions? On reflection, he considered it was only considered bad ton to show *real* emotion. A lady could not laugh out loud with pleasure, but she could give that high, chiming, artificial laugh taught by her music teacher. She could not betray either horror or disgust, but she was allowed to faint or cry genteelly to show sensibility. And passion? Never! Never was any lady supposed to burn and sigh and moan in his arms like Belinda Earle. And on that thought came a craving, a hunger, to see her again.

His valet slipped a night-gown over the marquess's

head, saw his master into bed, and then retired, slipping out of the room as soft-footed as a cat.

Why can I not see her again? thought the marquess suddenly. This is ridiculous. She is young, unmarried, and of good family.

He began to make plans. First he must get rid of the Jordans.

The Jordans rose early, or rather, early for them. Nine o'clock and the castle was resounding with scrapes and bangs and thumps. The smell of paint was everywhere.

Struggling into his dressing-gown, Sir Henry rang the bell and demanded testily to know what the deuce the infernal row was all about.

The chambermaid bobbed a curtsy and said his lordship was having every room redecorated.

'He can't!' wailed Lady Henry, sitting up in bed, her nightcap askew. 'Penelope!' For their darling daughter was highly sensitive to the smell of fresh paint.

Sir Henry dressed at great speed and went in search of the marquess. There seemed to be paint-pots and ladders and workmen everywhere.

'Ah, Sir Henry,' called the marquess cheerfully as that gentleman ran him to earth in the breakfast-room.

'You must send all these decorators away,' said Sir Henry wrathfully. 'The smell of paint makes my poor Penelope ill.'

The marquess affected concern. 'My dear Sir Henry. What am I to do? It is hard for the local artisans to find work in the winter. I cannot cut off their employ. But as I am leaving shortly, it might be a good idea if you started on your journey as well.'

'But you have not yet proposed to my daughter, or have you?' barked Sir Henry, almost beside himself with fury and thwarted hope.

The marquess's eyes went quite blank. 'I have not yet proposed to your daughter, nor shall I. I fear I am a confirmed bachelor.'

'You led us to believe the knot was as good as tied.'

'I did no such thing.'

'Damme, that trolley I bought you at great expense, mark you, at *great expense*, was by way of an engagement present.'

The marquess turned to the butler, who was standing by the sideboard. 'Hemmings,' he said, 'take said trolley from the dining-room, parcel it up, and give it back to Sir Henry; or better still, put it in his carriage with his baggage and have his carriage brought round to the front door in readiness. Unfortunately, Sir Henry finds himself obliged to leave.'

'Pah!' said Sir Henry, hopping up and down in rage and disappointment. 'Pah, pah, and pooh to you, sir!'

The marquess picked up the morning paper and began to read it.

It was hard to tell, when the Jordans left, whether Penelope was crying with rage or weeping from the effects of the paint. Her eyes were red and swollen.

'I shall never forgive her. Never!' said Penelope as the carriage drove off.

'Who?' asked her mother.

'That Belinda Earle creature and her sluttish ways.'

'Put it all out of your mind,' said Lady Jordan. 'Frenton is quite mad. Have you your book, Sir Henry?'

'Already looking,' muttered Sir Henry. He kept a book of all the noble families with eligible sons and their addresses. 'Here it is,' he said at last. 'Lord Frederick, eldest son of the Earl of Twitterton. They have a box between Shepherd's Shore and Devizes. You have not met Lord Frederick, Penelope. He is returned from the Grand Tour this month. We shall strike while the iron is hot.'

The marquess, having started the decoration to get rid of the Jordans, decided to go ahead with it and stayed to supervise. Miss Earle would be at the inn close at hand for the next few days. Having made up his mind to see her again, caution set in and he decided he did not want to appear too eager. He did not know her very well, after all.

But, unknown to him, by the following morning the Bath coach was once more on the road. Belinda's heart plummetted as the coach slowly rolled out of the inn yard. He had not come. He was probably engaged to chilly Penelope by now.

She was relieved that the odious Mr Biles at least had the merit of making Miss Wimple his concern. He fussed over her and handed her smelling-salts and read to her. She fluttered and tittered and thanked him profusely. She appeared to be in prime health and despite her fondness for spirits was evidently as strong as an ox.

118

Hannah passed the tedium of the journey by regaling Belinda with tales from the guidebook. When they reached Beckhampton, where the Bath roads converged, Belinda was disappointed that they were only to be allowed half an hour, for she had hoped to see the abbey nearby. Hannah had told her a most intriguing story about it. Evidently, in the sixteenth century, there lived a young lady called Miss Sheringham whose father owned the abbey. She had been refused permission to see her lover, one John Talbot. One night she was standing on the abbey battlements calling down to him. Then she said, 'I will leap down to you,' a rather unwise decision as the walls were thirty feet high. Nonetheless, she leaped. The wind came to her rescue and 'got under her coates' (no doubt, the ulster of the sixteenth century), and so assisted, she flopped down into the arms of Talbot and to all appearances killed him dead on the spot. She sat down and wept. But Talbot, who had only been temporarily winded, recovered and clasped her in his arms. And it was at that point that Miss Sheringham's father, with a fine sense of the melodramatic, jumped out of a bush and observed, 'as his daughter had made such a leap to him, she must e'en marry him.' And so they were married and lived happily ever after.

Belinda could not share Hannah's enthusiasm for coach travel. Despite the sunny weather, the coach was cold and damp. It had been vigorously hosed down inside after its repairs and did not seem to have dried out. The constant swaying was making her feel sick. She had started her journey hoping it would take as long as possible. Now she felt even Great-Aunt Harriet would be preferable. Every time she thought of the Marquess of Frenton, which was frequently, she felt so low in spirits that she believed there was nothing left anyone could do to lower them any further. At the inn at Beckhampton, there had been a party of bloods from another coach and they had been discoursing loudly and anatomically about the charms of a certain Sally until the horrified landlord had turned them out. Belinda shuddered as she wondered whether the marquess would tell *his* friends about her vulgar passions.

Bath was drawing even closer. The coachman was a good and steady man and the horses were fresh. But three and a half miles outside Beckhampton they crossed high, windy, unprotected ground. The temperature had been dropping rapidly, and to the dismay of the passengers, they found that snow had begun to fall.

They stopped at a tiny inn called Shepherd's Shore and all crowded around the fire. The coachman said he thought they should all stay where they were until the storm had passed, but the Methodist minister, Mr Biles, had grown as brave as only half a bottle of good Nantes brandy can make a normally weak man and overrode the coachman and the others by saying this was the last stage before Bath and as soon as they descended to lower ground, the snow would turn to rain. The coachman demurred at first, but he knew the coach was already days late and so he reluctantly agreed to take them forward.

They only got a mile from Shepherd's Shore when the full force of the storm struck. The coachman cursed himself for his folly in having listened to the drunken minister. He did not want to lose his job, as had the previous coachman, by causing more harm to befall the passengers. He saw dimly through the blinding snow a tall pair of iron gates. The guard blew on the horn and a lodge-keeper came out and swung the gates open.

'Residence?' called the coachman to the lodge-keeper.

'Earl o' Twitterton,' replied the lodge-keeper.

'His lordship's in for some unexpected guests,' muttered the coachman, and cracking the whip, he urged his team of horses up the long, wintry drive to the Earl of Twitterton's home.

6

Had Belinda still been at the inn, the marquess might have begun to wonder at the folly of calling on her. But by the time he arrived at the Queen Bess, it was to learn the stage-coach had left.

He was as annoyed as if Belinda had deliberately avoided him. He returned to the castle, ordered his travelling carriage, and set out in pursuit. He traced them as far as Beckhampton to find they had left an hour before and learned they would probably be stopping next at Shepherd's Shore.

He drove on, and as the ground began to rise, so he found himself enveloped in the same snowstorm that had beset the passengers. They were not at Shepherd's Shore and he wondered whether this stage coachman was as crazy as the last had been and had forged on to Bath. He began to worry, seeing in his mind's eye Belinda lying in a snow-drift, calling for help.

He came to the lodge-gates and remembered that the Earl of Twitterton had a hunting-box there. He stopped and inquired at the lodge and was told that the stage-coach had gone up to the house.

He was driving the carriage himself. His valet was warmly ensconced inside and one complaining tiger hung on the backstrap.

The marquess jumped down and told his tiger to take carriage and horses to the stables. The snow was still falling fast, but it had become wetter and the air was perceptibly warmer.

He presented his card to the butler, who answered the door. The earl himself came out to meet him. He was a bluff, soldierly man who had met the marquess before on several occasions and gave him a warm welcome, not asking the reason for the unexpected visit, assuming the marquess was taking shelter from the storm.

The earl said they had already dined and that the servants would prepare something for him, but the marquess had eaten a hasty meal at Beckhampton and so he said he would change out of his travelling clothes and then join the family. As his valet laid out his evening clothes and powdered his master's hair, the marquess wondered how Belinda would look when she saw him again. Would she blush? Would she look angry? No doubt the stern Miss Pym had read her a lecture on the folly of her ways.

He found to his surprise that he was nervous. A footman led the way down to the first floor, saying the family and guests were in the drawing-room.

The double doors were thrown wide and the marquess's name was announced. The marquess raised his quizzing-glass and studied the faces turned towards him. His heart sank.

The earl's son, Lord Frederick, a brutish-looking young man, was standing by the fireplace. Seated beside the fire was Penelope Jordan. On a sofa, side by side, were her parents, both glaring at him. In a corner was some sort of poor relation, a faded lady netting a purse. The Countess of Twitterton rose to meet him. She was a thin, hard, horsy woman, wearing a row of false curls over her forehead. She should not have gained such a name by marriage as Twitterton, thought the earl. 'Twitterton' suggested a vague, dithering sort of female. The countess should have been called 'Basher' or 'Floggem'. She looked like a man masquerading as a woman.

She was an excellent shot, the marquess remembered, and killed anything furred or feathered with a deadly aim. Perhaps that was why this drawing-room, albeit a drawing-room in a hunting-box, did not show any feminine frills or china. Trophies of the countess's hunting prowess stared glassily down from the walls. All the animals she had killed looked as if they had died in a fit of boredom. There were also various bad oil paintings of slaughtered game. There was one painting of the countess herself over the fireplace. She was dressed in a filmy blue gown, her hair powdered. The artist had done his best to romanticize his subject, painting broken columns in the background, a Greek temple, and an approaching thunderstorm. But he had painted the expression in her eyes perfectly so that the painted countess surveyed the gathering in much the same way as the real-life one was doing – with a hard, autocratic, judgemental stare.

'Didn't think a little bit of snow would drive you off the road, Frenton,' she said. 'May I introduce ... ?'

'I already know the Jordan family,' said the marquess. Penelope struck an Attitude. It was meant to represent The Broken Heart. She put one hand on her bosom, stretched the other hand out and cast her eyes up to the ceiling.

'Got indigestion, Miss Jordan?' demanded the countess. 'Rhubarb pills, that's the thing. Shouldn't have, though. Got a splendid chef, Frenton. That venison we had for dinner was hung till the maggots were crawling out of it. Sit down, Frenton. How's hunting?'

'I don't know,' said the marquess. 'Don't hunt.'

'But your papa kept the best pack in the county!'

'One of his many extravagances,' murmured the marquess. He looked around pointedly. 'The lodge-keeper told me the stage-coach had descended on you.'

'Yes, and a confounded nuisance it was, too.'

'Hah,' said Sir Henry in a voice he hoped was laden with sarcasm. 'Ha! Ho!'

'And where are the passengers?' asked the marquess.

'In the kitchens where they belong.'

'Is the coach The Quicksilver?'

'Yes,' said the countess. 'Why?'

'They took refuge with me for a few days.'

'There you are,' said the earl. 'Just proves what I'm always saying. This stage-coach business has got to stop. Not only does it allow the common people freedom to move hither and thither about the countryside, but come a little bit of bad weather, and they think they have the right to thrust their noses inside the door of every noble mansion.'

'You are behind the times,' said the marquess. 'It is not only commoners who use the stage-coach.'

'Go along with you,' said the countess. 'This lot's got a Methody among 'em.'

'I escaped that pleasure,' said the marquess. 'I entertained them as guests.'

'With no concern whatsoever for my daughter's feelings,' barked Sir Henry. 'Told you so.'

'You don't need to do that sort of thing any more, Frenton,' said Lord Frederick.

'What sort of thing?'

'Well, let a lot of commoners put their thick boots under your dining-table, don't you see. I mean, it was different when we thought the French Terror would spread over here, but they ain't going to rise up and hang us from the lamp-posts, so we don't need to be pleasant to 'em any more. And a damned good thing, too. Beg pardon, ladies.'

'How refreshingly unsophisticated you all are,' said the marquess. He raised his quizzing-glass, studied the cut of Lord Frederick's coat, and sadly shook his head. 'Now I am not so high in the instep, and by having these stage-coach people in my company, I found a treasure.'

'Going too far. Too far,' roared Sir Henry.

The marquess treated him to an icy stare. 'By which I mean I discovered two of the best voices in the country.'

The countess regarded him suspiciously. 'Mean that opera caterwauling?'

'Anything you like,' said the marquess. 'They have an enormous repertoire.'

'Have 'em up,' said Lord Frederick. 'Bit of fun. Bit of a lark, hey?'

Lady Jordan stepped into the breach. 'I do not think you would enjoy these persons' company *at all.*'

The countess, who had been about to refuse to send for the passengers, turned contrary and glared at Lady Jordan. 'I'll have 'em here if I want.'

Belinda and the passengers were eating a late supper in the servants' hall. They all knew the Jordans were staying as guests. Belinda was glad that they were confined belowstairs.

It was therefore with a sinking heart that she heard the summons from the butler that they were all, except the coachman and guard, to go up to the drawing-room.

She smoothed down the creases in her gown as she stood up. She wished there were some way she could change into evening dress, but the butler was waiting impatiently and so, keeping very close to Hannah, she mounted the stairs.

When she reached the drawing-room, she half-turned to flee. There was the Marquess of Frenton, there the Jordans. They must have come together, thought Belinda. He must mean to marry her if he has started taking her about with him on visits.

Penelope was wearing a white silk slip of a gown with a silver gauze overdress fastened with gold clasps. A heavy gold-and-garnet necklace emphasized the whiteness of her throat and her glossy brown curls were bound by a gold filet. Her gown was looped over her arm as she stood up, revealing a surprisingly thick leg and shapeless ankle. A thin ray of sunlight shone into the gloom of Belinda's mind as she saw that leg. Also, Belinda had taken off her pelisse before leaving the kitchen and knew that her muslin morning gown was ruffed and vandyked with the finest lace, and for almost the first time she took comfort in the armour of expensive fashion.

The marquess made the introductions. 'Yes, yes,' said the countess impatiently. 'Which are the singers?' The Judds edged forward, holding hands.

'Then sing!' commanded the countess, waving her hand imperiously towards a spinet in the corner. Hannah went with them and pretended to be helping them by lighting the candles that stood on top. 'Sing something John Bullish and patriotic,' she hissed.

She returned and took a seat in the corner next to the poor relation, who turned out to be a Miss Forbes, a fourth cousin of the countess.

'I do hope they don't put Lady Twitterton in a taking,' whispered Miss Forbes. 'When she was but a gel, she threw a vase of flowers at an Italian opera singer's head.'

And indeed, it did look as if the countess was regretting her invitation. 'One song and that's that,' she muttered in an aside to her son.

This time it was Mrs Judd who played the accompaniment. Mr Judd stood with one hand in his waistcoat pocket and the other resting on the edge of the spinet. He threw back his head, stuck out his chest, and began to sing:

'Come, cheer up, my lads! 'Tis to glory we steer,
To add something more to this wonderful year;
To honour we call you, not press you like slaves,
For who are so free as the sons of the waves?'

The Judds looked considerably taken aback, but then delighted as the Earl and Countess of Twitterton and their son began to roar out the chorus. Hannah saw the stark disapproval on the Jordan family's faces and gleefully prepared to join in.

'Heart of oak are our ships,' screeched the countess.

'Heart of oak are our men,' bawled the earl.

'We always are ready; Steady boys, steady,' roared Lord Frederick in a deep bass.

And then the Twitterton family, Hannah, Miss Wimple, Mr Biles, Belinda, and the marquess all joined together in the last of the refrain:

'We'll fight and we'll conquer again and again.'

Mr Judd's performance was cheered. Much emboldened, he went on to sing: 'Oh, the roast beef of England, And England's roast beef!'

The countess was noisy in her delight and called to Mrs Judd to sing something. Hannah almost held her breath. She hoped Mrs Judd would not sing something operatic. To her relief, Mrs Judd threw a rather saucy look at the earl and began to sing merrily:

'A Captain bold, in Halifax, who dwelt in
    country quarters,
Seduced a maid who hanged herself, one
    morning in her garters,
His wicked conscience smited him, he lost his
    stomach daily,
He took to drinking ratafee, and thought upon
    Miss Bailey.
Oh, Miss Bailey! unfortunate Miss Bailey.'

Then, when the company had finished laughing at the plight of Miss Bailey's ghost, Mrs Judd sang a sentimental ballad. This, too, pleased the countess immensely.

Penelope looked covertly at Belinda Earle. But the girl was still not beautiful at all; in fact, she looked crushed and diminished. Why was it then that Frenton appeared to be trying to seem unaware of her and Lord Frederick kept beaming at Belinda with a silly smile on his face? Then, horror of horrors, Lord Frederick left his post by the fire-place and drew up a chair next to Belinda's. Before the arrival of the marquess and these hell-sent stage-coach passengers Lord Frederick had been behaving with Penelope just as he ought. He had paid court to her beauty and found every opportunity to be in her company.

Penelope could not know what was going on in Lord Frederick's rather simple brain. He had been thinking what a rare treat this evening must be for a common lady like Belinda and how she would no doubt cherish it forever and talk to her grandchildren in later years about the evening she spent in a noble household. It made him feel grand and sort of Lord Bountiful-ish. In a pause in the musical recital, he asked Belinda what she thought of the hunting-box. Her reply startled him. 'It always amazes me,' said Belinda, 'that a building called a mere "box" should always be so very large and grand. Mind you, my lord, I have only stayed at one before and that was at Lord Bellamy's near Nottingham.'

'Coach break down there as well?' he asked sympathetically.

'Oh, no,' said Belinda. 'Lord Bellamy is my great-uncle.'

'Haven't seen Bellamy this age,' said Lord Frederick, barely able to believe her.

'He died last year,' said Belinda. 'My Great-Aunt Harriet, Lady Bellamy, lives in The Bath, and it is there that I am bound.'

He looked at her doubtfully. 'I have heard of ladies travelling by the stage because it saves the expense of out-riders, postilions and goodness knows how many other servants.'

'It was the decision of my uncle and aunt to send me by the stage,' said Belinda.

'How came it you landed in at Baddell Castle? Pole break?'

'No, worse than that,' said Belinda. 'The driver was drunk and fell asleep. The coach left the road and we landed in the middle of a river. It was there that the marquess found us.'

'Well, if that don't beat all. What an adventure. Were you hurt?'

'I sprained my ankle.' Belinda poked a neat foot forward to show him an ankle wrapped in a bandage.

'I say, you should rest that. Better get Mama to find you a bedchamber. Hey, Mother, this lady's hurt her ankle. If you ain't got any bedchambers made up, Miss Earle can have mine. She's old Bellamy's great-niece, by the way.'

'How is he?' asked the countess.

'Dead, my lady.'

'Sad. What of?'

'A seizure, my lady.'

'And what of that moralizing wife of his?'

'At The Bath, my lady. I am to stay with her.'

'Sorry for you and that's a fact.' The countess fell silent, for the Judds were preparing to sing again. They sang several popular duets and rounded off their recital with a rousing rendition of 'Rule, Britannia!'

Amid the noisy applause, the countess strode over to the piano and accosted them. She began to question them about themselves and, on finding out all about the seminary, and then about the Marquess of

Frenton's introductions, an idea hit her. She knew that her peers considered her an eccentric and the only way she could ever outshine anyone was on the hunting field, but since only ladies of her own rather masculine stamp hunted, there was not much of a feeling of success in that. But if she could produce these singing Judds in her own drawing-room in the town house in London as *her* find, she would be able to put a good few aristocratic noses out of joint. Overwhelmed with gratitude, the Judds breathlessly agreed. Satisfied and delighted with their gratitude, the countess rang the bell and ordered bedchambers to be made ready for the stage-coach passengers whom she had previously expected to bed down on the floor of the servants' hall.

The marquess was wondering what to do. He wanted to talk to Belinda but she was being monopolized by Lord Frederick. His eyes drifted over the assembled company. Miss Wimple, wearing a tremendous turban to disguise her shaven head, was talking in a low voice to the Methodist minister. The marquess studied the minister and his eyes sharpened. Hannah, watching from her corner, noticed that Mr Biles saw the marquess looking at him and the way Mr Biles flushed and averted his eyes.

Penelope at that moment caught Lord Frederick's eye and beckoned to him. With a hurried excuse to Belinda, he rose and went to join her. The marquess took his vacated seat.

'I am pleased to see you again, Miss Earle,' he began.

Belinda bowed her head but made no reply. Her eye-lashes were very long and silky, the marquess noticed. Belinda Earle was like a good painting that one could examine at length and each time discover something new and pleasing. 'I was on my way to The Bath,' he said, unable to bring himself to say that the sole reason for his journey was to look for her. 'I was very surprised to find the Jordan family here.'

Belinda looked at him, startled. 'I had assumed you came with them!'

'No, unfortunately they had to leave the castle.'

She had a sudden hope that he had sent them packing. 'Why?'

'Because I am having all the rooms redecorated and, alas, Miss Jordan is made quite ill by the smell of fresh paint.'

Meanwhile, Lord Frederick was telling a highly irritated Penelope about Belinda's good social standing. 'Odd, is it not?' he asked.

'What is odd?' snapped Penelope.

'That Miss Earle should choose to travel by the stage.'

'There is a great deal odd about Miss Earle,' said Penelope, lowering her voice. 'Do you know she had the temerity to make an assignation with the Marquess of Frenton?'

'When? Where?'

'She sent him a letter. My maid told me of it and I thought I had better warn that travelling companion of hers, Miss Pym, about it as her real companion was ill. But Miss Pym, as far as I can guess, did nothing. Miss Earle is a well-known hussy.'

'How shocking,' said Lord Frederick. 'Thought Frenton was courting you, or rather, that's what the gossips said.'

'He was,' said Penelope in a sad voice. 'But I asked Mama and Papa to take me away, for I fear I and the marquess would not suit. He is a trifle old and set in his ways.' She cast Lord Frederick a languishing look. 'I prefer younger men.'

'By George! And so you should, a delightful beauty like yourself, Miss Jordan.'

Lord Frederick's brain, usually not very agile, appeared all at once to be working at a great rate. He had every intention of proposing to Penelope. She was rich and she was beautiful, and he could not understand why she had not been snapped up before. Lord Frederick was very much a man of his age. Love and marriage in his opinion definitely did not mix. One needed a pretty wife to grace one's bed and table, but real pleasure was to be found elsewhere. He paid Penelope further compliments while his hot eyes ranged in the direction of Belinda Earle. He was sure she was the reason the marquess had pretended to need shelter from the storm. On to a good thing, too, thought Lord Frederick. He himself wouldn't mind getting a leg over that. Young and sweet and, what was more important, no fear of the pox. Might try his luck with her himself.

The marquess, by talking on general topics and showing her every mark of respect, was trying to repair the damage he must have surely done in treating Belinda so vulgarly.

Belinda replied automatically, her spirits very low. It was obvious to her that the marquess had only kissed her because he thought she was damaged goods. When he had found out she was not, he had decided she was like any other boring female of his acquaintance, someone to talk civilities to. She did not know that behind the marquess's calm eyes his brain was furiously working out some way in which he could get a chance to kiss that glorious mouth again. He was not yet sure whether he wanted to marry her.

The countess interrupted their conversation, asking the marquess again why he did not hunt, and Belinda was left with her thoughts. Penelope was flirting with Lord Frederick. How could she? marvelled Belinda. Lord Frederick, despite his fine evening clothes, had a low forehead and a leering, nasty look about the eyes. But Penelope was glowing and her beauty gave Belinda another sharp stab of jealousy.

Belinda furtively fingered her own thin, finely arched eyebrows and then looked miserably at Penelope's thick, luxuriant ones. Also, as Penelope raised an arm to adjust a curl, she revealed a strong bush of hair growing in her armpit.

It was an age when gentlemen preferred ladies to have a lot of hair – everywhere. Never had false hair been in such demand. Not only should the hair on one's head be thick and luxuriant, but the eyebrows were supposed to be thick, and the arms and the armpits seductively hairy. Some ladies, Belinda had heard, even shaved their arms regularly in the hope of encouraging growth. The newspapers abounded with notices advertising not only wigs but false eyebrows, and there were even advertisements for pubic wigs, complete with illustrations, there for anyone to see. Belinda saw the marquess looking at her and blushed deep red. No young lady should even *think* about pubic hair.

Hannah Pym was now holding a skein of wool for the poor relation. She saw the way Penelope leaned forward intimately to talk to Lord Frederick and then the way that gentleman's eyes widened and he stared across the room at Belinda.

Hannah glared at Miss Wimple. She blamed the companion for starting all the gossip about Belinda, forgetting in her distress that it was Belinda herself who had given Penelope suspicions about the innocence of her character by writing that letter to Frenton. Damn Miss Wimple, thought Hannah. If only she would get really drunk and disgrace herself. But she was so taken up with that Methodist minister that she was behaving like a virginal miss in her teens.

Finally, the countess rose as a signal that the evening was at an end. Belinda, Hannah and Miss Wimple found they were to have a room each, the hunting-box having plenty of bedchambers so as to accommodate quite large parties of huntsmen.

Hannah would have preferred a room next to Belinda's but found she was in the floor above. She decided to read one of her guidebooks before going to bed. A hush had descended on the house. Hannah read on and then decided Belinda was safe for the night. If only the girl could avoid the marquess for a little longer; Hannah was sure Frenton would propose to her.

Belinda, too, was reluctant to sleep. The marquess had looked as if there were many things he wanted to say to her. Perhaps he would call on her. And yet if he did, it meant he was of the same mind as before. He thought she was easy game.

At last she blew out the light and settled herself for sleep. One moment, she thought it would never come, and the next, she had plunged down into oblivion.

The marquess was having a painful interview with Mr Biles, the Methodist minister. 'I do not think,' said the marquess, feeling pompous, 'that you are setting a good example to Miss Earle by flirting with her companion when you are a married man.' Mr Biles turned red and then white and then looked sulky. Mr Biles, the marquess knew, lived in a village some ten miles from the castle. He was a wealthy man, son of a prosperous tradesman, and had married the daughter of an equally wealthy tradesman some six months ago. The daughter had been a middle-aged spinster when Mr Biles led her to the altar. She was a fat, plain, rather argumentative woman. It had been assumed her generous dowry had been the attraction, but the marquess was now not so sure. Mr Biles seemed genuinely smitten by the unlikely charms of Miss Wimple, shaven head and all.

'I am sorry for Miss Wimple. I feel she has an onerous task,' said Mr Biles defiantly. 'Miss Earle–'

'That's enough!' snapped the marquess. 'Not one

word. Miss Earle is a highly respectable young lady. Miss Wimple should be more mindful of her duties and guard her tongue.'

Trembling with outrage, the Methodist minister drew himself up to his full height of five feet two inches. 'Miss Wimple is a precious pearl,' he said. 'I would do nothing to harm her. Just because you have a title and lands, you have no call to interfere in my life. You think you can walk over everyone. I, sir, am a Methodist and proud of it. I am not of the Church of England and need not fawn on every lord in the hope of a high living or a bishopric. I spurn you and all you stand for.'

'Miss Wimple,' said the marquess with a reluctant feeling of admiration for the minister's sudden access of dignity, 'is nonetheless a dangerous gossip. She does not have the interests of her charge at heart. On my arrival in The Bath, I have no other option but to call on Lady Bellamy, Miss Earle's great-aunt, and tell her I consider Miss Wimple unfit for the position she holds. Good night!'

He walked back to his own bedchamber, but before he reached it, he saw Lord Frederick, in his night-gown, tiptoeing along the corridor. To the marquess's amazement, Lord Frederick stopped at Belinda's door, turned the handle and walked in.

The marquess quickened his step and grasped hold of that young man by the shoulder just as he was approaching the sleeping figure on the bed.

'Wrong bedchamber,' said the marquess icily, swinging Lord Frederick around.

Belinda gave an exclamation and sat up in bed.

Lord Frederick was holding a candle in a flat stick. The light from it illumined the two men's faces.

Lord Frederick leered. 'Sorry if I'm spoiling your game, Frenton.'

The marquess punched him full on the mouth and Lord Frederick went flying. The candle hit the floor and went out.

Belinda scrabbled feverishly with the tinder-box beside the bed and lit her candle.

Lord Frederick was struggling to his feet with a villainous look in his eyes.

'You took me by surprise, you rat,' he said. 'Put up your fives.'

'Come outside,' said the marquess. 'We cannot brawl in a lady's bedchamber.'

'Here and now,' roared Lord Frederick. 'I don't care what your doxy thinks.'

The marquess struck him again, this time on the nose, and Lord Frederick reeled back.

'Stop it!' screamed Belinda. 'You are waking the whole household.'

Lord Frederick lurched purposefully towards the marquess, blood from his nose staining the white front of his night-gown.

Suddenly Belinda's bedchamber seemed to be full of people. Hannah was there, as were the Judds, the countess and earl, the Jordans, and several servants.

'What are the pair of you doing, punching each other in the middle of the night?' demanded the countess.

'I found Lord Frederick in my fiancée's bedchamber,' said the marquess calmly, 'and took appropriate action.'

Belinda blinked at him in a dazed way.

There was a sudden silence. Then Sir Henry Jordan gave tongue. 'Do you mean to tell me you were courting my daughter while you were already engaged to this . . . to this . . . ?'

'Careful,' warned the marquess.

'Oh, Lord Frederick,' cried Penelope. 'You are hurt. I cannot bear it.'

She swayed and then neatly fell into his arms. 'The deuce,' said Lord Frederick, pushing her into her mother's arms. 'Let me get at him.'

'Stop it, both of you,' ordered the countess, 'and tell me what this is all about. Frederick! What are you doing in Miss Earle's bedchamber?'

Lord Frederick opened his mouth and shut it again. Then he raised the hem of his night-gown and mopped his streaming nose. Penelope screamed and averted her eyes. The truculence was dying out of Lord Frederick's face and he was beginning to look puzzled.

'Demne,' he said, scratching his head, 'looks like I got hold of the wrong end of the stick. Miss Jordan told me this evening that Miss Earle was no better than she should be, and so I decided to try for a bit of sport. Then when Frenton walked in, stands to reason I thought Miss Earle was his . . . er . . . little friend, if you take my meaning. Now Frenton says he's engaged to her.' He rounded on Penelope. 'Why did you tell me such a hum?'

'They cannot be engaged,' gasped Penelope. 'They only met the other week for the first time.'

'It was love at first sight,' said the marquess in an expressionless voice. 'I am sorry I hit you, Frederick, but you were misled. My fiancée has suffered enough upset and distress. I suggest you go to bed and let me talk to her.'

'There's something havey-cavey in all this,' protested the earl. 'You never said anything about being engaged to Miss Earle when you arrived, and yet you must have known she was one of the stage-coach passengers.'

'I am of a shy nature,' said the marquess, 'and my love for Miss Earle made me even more shy. Besides, I was stricken with remorse at having let her travel ahead on the stage in this weather.'

Belinda sat up in bed, unable to move or speak. The sheer gladness that had flooded her body when he had first said she was his fiancée was quickly ebbing away. The marquess's eyes held a mocking glint now. He was making fools of the Twittertons and the Jordans, that was all.

One by one they all went out, all except Hannah Pym, who stood her ground.

'You, too, Miss Pym,' said the marquess.

'Are you really engaged?' asked Hannah.

'Yes,' said the marquess.

'No,' squeaked Belinda.

'So,' said Hannah, folding her arms, 'what is going on?'

The marquess sighed impatiently. All he wanted was to be shot of Hannah Pym and to kiss Belinda

Earle's delicious mouth. He had said Belinda was his fiancée on the spur of the moment and to save her reputation. But now it seemed like an excellent idea. He would have Belinda Earle and that mouth of hers for his sole property for the rest of his life and he found the idea enchanting. On the other hand, he still felt guilty at having behaved towards Belinda in such an ungentlemanly way in the first place, and he *had* just made a noble gesture. So he opened his mouth and proceeded to put his foot in it.

'It was all I could think of,' he said. 'Frederick has obviously been misled by Miss Jordan's malicious and jealous gossip, although when I first saw Frederick entering here, I thought Miss Wimple might have had a hand in it. I had to save Miss Earle's reputation, and so I said she was my fiancée.'

Belinda groaned and sank down on the pillows and drew the blankets over her head.

'So now what are you going to do?' asked Hannah.

'Why, marry her, of course!'

'Does she want to marry you?'

The marquess looked at Hannah in blank amazement. When did any woman *not* want to marry a wealthy marquess?

'Go on, ask her, while I am still here,' said Hannah grimly.

The marquess approached the bed. He tugged down the covers. Belinda's furious eyes glared up at him. 'Will you marry me?' he asked.

'No, I will not,' said Belinda, and jerked the covers up over her face again.

The marquess swung round. 'Do leave us, Miss Pym. Miss Earle is not your concern.'

'No, I will not, sirrah. Miss Earle does not want you and so I shall stay right here until you leave.'

Belinda heard Hannah's words, and instead of being grateful to her, she was suddenly and irrationally furious. Was her life always going to be dogged by middle-aged people who did not think she had a mind of her own?

She struggled up from under the blankets again. 'I can fight my own battles, Miss Pym. Pray do as his lordship requires.'

'I cannot argue with you, Miss Earle,' said Hannah severely. 'But I am going to fetch Miss Wimple. You *are* her concern and she should be here.'

Hannah marched out but left the door open.

Belinda surveyed the marquess with a militant eye. He was still in his evening dress and his hair was powdered. His eyes looked aloof and remote. 'Well?' demanded Belinda sarcastically. 'Tell me all about this love at first sight.'

He sat down on the bed and looked down at her. 'I was trying to save your reputation.'

'Good!' said Belinda, her eyes flashing. 'Now you have done that . . . go away.'

It was obviously the moment to tell her he loved her, but his pride would not let him. He had already been made too vulnerable by this girl who could wrench his heart-strings so easily. She did not love him, he thought sadly, or she would not look so contemptuous and angry.

Then he began to find himself becoming angry. There was that mouth, just below his. He put his hands on either side of her body and leaned down. He bent his head . . . and passionately kissed a mouthful of blanket. Belinda had dived under the covers again. He stood up and stripped the covers off her and threw them on the floor. He knelt on one knee on the bed, grasped the front of her night-gown and jerked her up against him. 'Now, you will kiss me,' he said.

Belinda opened her mouth to scream. He covered her mouth with his own and began to kiss her with single-minded intensity. Belinda beat at his shoulders and then pulled at his powdered hair, giving it several painful yanks, but he had the rest of her body and mouth imprisoned. The hand holding the front of her gown was pressed tightly against her breast. Her body was turning to liquid fire and her lips were beginning to tremble beneath his own.

Hannah Pym stood in the doorway again. For a short moment, shock kept her silent. Such blatant passion was indecent. They were both alike. They must get married and leave the world safe for decent people who did not know the meaning of lust.

'My lord!' she called loudly.

The marquess dropped Belinda on the bed and then looked at Hannah with a basilisk stare. Hannah felt her authority shrivel before that stare. Hannah, the gentlewoman of independent means, fled; even Hannah, the housekeeper ruling over a large staff, melted away. She could feel herself back in the kitchens of Thornton House as a scullery maid. She felt like apologizing for her very existence, and only Duty, stern daugher of the voice of God, made her give herself a mental shake and say in a strong voice, 'They've gone; fled. Miss Wimple and Mr Biles, and a footman tells me they've taken the earl's carriage!'

'Good riddance,' said the marquess.

Hannah's eyes flew to Belinda. Belinda was looking the picture of shame. If he had told her he loved her, she would be radiant. Men! thought Hannah bitterly.

'Why have they gone?' asked Hannah. 'They had no need to flee.'

'They had every need, madam,' said the marquess. 'Mr Biles is already married.'

'Married? Does Miss Wimple know?'

'I doubt it.'

'But we must save her,' said Belinda.

'My dear heart,' he said in a testy voice that robbed the words of any affection, 'you are rid of a companion who did her best to blacken your name.'

'I do not like her,' said Belinda. 'But I am going to try to find her. I cannot stand by and see even such as Miss Wimple ruined. She does not have much money, and if he abandons her there is nothing left for a lady to do but to go on the streets.'

'Might stop her damned moralizing,' said the marquess savagely.

'We will all go,' said Hannah soothingly. 'My lord no doubt has a carriage.'

'Which is staying in the stables.'

'Which you will get out of the stables,' said Hannah,

'unless, of course, you have no affection for Miss Earle whatsoever.'

He looked at her in silence. Hannah met his gaze steadily. Hannah did not care a rap what happened to Miss Wimple, but she was frightened to leave matters between Belinda and the marquess as they were. If Belinda was allowed to go ahead on the coach to The Bath in the morning, then perhaps by the time the Marquess of Frenton should be calling on that moralizing great-aunt to ask permission to pay his addresses, he might instead have been snapped up by some designing female. And Hannah did believe that it was never any good for the path of true love to run smooth.

The marquess looked at Belinda. Her face was flushed and her hair tumbled and he realized with a shock that he found her very beautiful indeed and doubted that he would ever think of her as an ordinary-looking female again.

'Very well,' he said. 'I will change into my travelling clothes. Miss Pym, I suggest you go to the servants' hall and tell the coachman that neither you, Miss Earle, Miss Wimple, or Mr Biles will be taking the stage. Oh, and I gather the Judds are to remain here. He will have an empty coach. Give me half an hour and then meet me in the hall!'

7

Oh heav'nly fool, thy most kiss-worthy face
Anger invests with such a lovely grace,
That Anger's self I needs must kiss again.

Sir Philip Sidney

'They will have headed for the city,' said the marquess, meaning Bath. 'We shall go in that direction first.'

He helped the ladies into the carriage and climbed up on the box. Hannah was disappointed. She had not expected the marquess to drive his carriage himself. She had hoped the couple would have had the opportunity to talk to each other on the journey and get to know each other better. Hugs and kisses were all very well, thought Hannah, giving her nose a tug. But how would they ever find out if they were suited if they never had a chance to talk?

'Do you think he is angry with us?' ventured

Belinda, peering out into the snow-covered blackness. Although the snow had stopped falling, the countryside was white.

'For going in search of Miss Wimple? He was at first, but now I think he is reconciled to it, and he must be glad to be shot of the Jordans, as are we all.'

'Did you mark that when Penelope Jordan joined the others in my bedchamber that her eyebrows were quite thin?'

'No, I did not,' said Hannah roundly. 'I had other things to think about.'

'Well, they were,' said Belinda triumphantly. 'And that means she wears false eyebrows.'

'A dangerous practice,' said Hannah severely. 'It is one to be avoided. Mrs Clarence gave a dinner party once and there was a certain Sir Brian Curtis and his lady present. Right in the middle of dinner, he roared across the table at his wife, "Your left eyebrow is slipping." Most mortifying for the lady. And then there was another gentleman who had strictly forbidden his wife to wear paint. She appeared in the drawing-room with a little rouge on her face. He grabbed a napkin, soaked it in seltzer, seized her, and scrubbed her face clean before the whole company.'

'How dreadful! It is just as well this business of me marrying Frenton is all a hum. Marriage is a state to be avoided if a female can afford it.'

'True,' said Hannah gloomily. 'Men *will* regard us as their chattels, you know, and . . . Faith! What am I saying? Not all men are thus, Miss Earle, I assure you. Furthermore, I do not think Frenton was teasing when he named you as his fiancée. There is his pride, you see.'

'And there is mine,' said Belinda. 'He would take my very soul away,' she said, half to herself.

Hannah fell silent. Belinda was left to think about the nature of love. Of course she had often thought about love, but had imagined that feeling would be something pure and spiritual. At that very moment, she hated the marquess, but at the same time longed for some sign of affection from him.

She peered out of the window of the carriage again. 'We are moving down to lower ground,' she said, 'and there is no snow and the road is quite dry. How odd the vagaries of the English climate! Although I am concerned for Miss Wimple, I am sharp set. I barely touched anything last evening. The venison was vile, stringy and gamy, and the smell!'

'I confess I could touch little of it myself. Moral people seem to have stomachs of iron. Both Miss Wimple and Mr Biles ate great quantities of the stuff. But as to Miss Wimple, it is our duty to apprise her of the facts because she is a woman and a fellow sufferer. If we women do not stick together, then what hope is there for us?'

'Have you never met a man with whom you could spend the rest of your life?' asked Belinda.

'There was one,' said Hannah, 'but he turned out to be a cheat and a liar and deceived me sore. Thank goodness that there *are* good men in this world.' She thought of Sir George Clarence with his fine figure, his piercing blue eyes, and the courteous way he listened to her so intently. He had offered to take her on a tour of the gardens of Thornton House on her return. Would he remember his offer? Perhaps he would marry and his new wife would frown on this strange friendship with a servant, albeit a former one. The thought of Sir George's marrying anyone depressed Hannah.

'The carriage is stopping,' she said.

'Perhaps we are going to be allowed something to eat,' remarked Belinda hopefully.

The marquess opened the carriage door. 'I am going to make inquiries at this inn.'

'Any hope of breakfast?' asked Belinda.

'Later,' he said shortly.

'You have the right of it, Miss Pym,' said Belinda bitterly when the marquess had closed the carriage door again. 'We must always do as we are told.'

'My fault,' said Hannah. 'Never ask a tentative question of a gentleman or the answer is bound to be no. I should have said, "Help us down. We are going to have breakfast."'

'That wouldn't have worked either,' said Belinda. 'Try it.'

After only a short time, the marquess returned. 'Good news,' he said. 'They stopped here and paid a driver handsomely to return the carriage and horses to the earl.'

'Did they go ahead on foot?' asked Belinda.

'No, they paid for a pony and gig and took off in that. They asked the road to Monks Parton.'

'And where is that?' asked Hannah.

'About six miles to the north.'

'Good,' said Belinda. 'Now, if you will but stand aside, my lord, I am going inside that hostelry with Miss Pym and we are going to have some breakfast.'

'As you will,' he said.

'There you are,' muttered Hannah gleefully. 'Works like a charm.'

Seated at a table in the coffee-parlour of the inn, Belinda and the marquess studied each other warily. Belinda thought the marquess, even in top-boots and a plain coat, looked more like a haughty aristocrat than ever, his cold eyes giving nothing away. The marquess wondered why Belinda, tired as she was, and with shadows under her eyes, looked like the most beautiful woman in the world, and then wondered whether she had bewitched him, but he showed all these confused thoughts and feelings like a true English gentleman by asking her, 'More coffee, Miss Earle?'

Hannah began to despair of the pair of them. Of course there were marriages where husband hardly ever spoke to wife, but such had been the marriage of Mr and Mrs Clarence, and only look where that had led. Her eyes glowed blue with remembered sadness.

'You are like a chameleon, Miss Pym,' said the marquess. 'I have observed your eyes change colour according to your mood.'

Hannah, who privately thought he would have done better to observe Belinda's eyes, replied, 'Humph,' and buried her nose in her coffee-cup.

'The sky will soon be light,' said the marquess, 'and

the morning promises to be fine. It should be an easy and pleasant journey to Monks Parton. I have plenty of carriage rugs. Would you care to wrap up well, Miss Earle, and join me on the box?'

Hannah feared that Belinda was on the point of saying something pettish and kicked her viciously in the ankle. Belinda let out a yelp of pain.

'What is the matter?' asked the marquess anxiously. 'Is it your ankle? I had forgot about that sprain.'

'I experienced a sudden twinge of pain in my other ankle,' said Belinda, glaring at Hannah. 'Yes, I would like to join you. I have never travelled on the box of a carriage before.'

Hannah smiled, well pleased.

After Belinda had been helped up on the box and wrapped in a bearskin rug, Hannah climbed inside, accompanied by the marquess's valet, curled up on the carriage seat and went to sleep.

'How very high above the ground we seem to be,' said Belinda nervously.

The team of grey horses ambled slowly forward. The air was sweet and there was a hint of spring in the warmth of the wind. Behind her the tiger, also wrapped in rugs, had fallen asleep.

'So I have you to myself at last,' said the marquess. 'I am sorry I did not make you a formal proposal of marriage, but the circumstances were odd. I shall call on your great-aunt when we reach The Bath.'

'But what do we know of each other?' demanded Belinda, looking at his hard profile. 'I had made up my mind not to marry, to be independent.'

'You would have independence were you married to me. A spinster has a sad life.'

'Miss Pym is a spinster.'

'True. But Miss Pym is an Original.'

'But you don't really want to marry me,' said Belinda. 'You were just being chivalrous.'

'Alas, I am never chivalrous.'

'Why do you want to marry me?'

The marquess reined in his horses and looked down at her angrily. 'Because I love you, dammit, as well you know.'

'No, I *don't* know,' snapped Belinda.

He dropped the reins and took her in his arms. 'Then let my silent lips tell you what my words cannot.' He kissed her tenderly on her eyes, her nose, and then her mouth. No more bruising kissing, thought the marquess. But Belinda freed her lips and looked up at him with starry eyes, and said with a break of laughter in her voice, 'Oh, you do love me, and I love you so much, Frenton.'

He crushed her close to him and sank his mouth into hers. Her passion rose to meet his. She caressed his hair and then choked and sneezed as a fine cloud of scented powder rose in the air.

'We had better be married very soon,' he said tenderly, handing her a large handkerchief.

'Yes,' agreed Belinda happily. 'And you do believe me, or rather you did believe Miss Pym when she told you the real story about that footman?'

'Yes, my love. Oh, yes, Belinda.'

'I do not know your first name,' said Belinda, shyly twisting a button on his coat.

154

'It is Richard. Say, "Richard, I love you."'

Her eyes were shining. 'Oh, Richard, my dear heart, I love you so much.'

He held her close. Their lips joined in a kiss of such intensity that for both the world seemed to spin round faster and faster about them.

Inside the carriage, Hannah Pym awoke and sat up. The carriage was at a standstill. Perhaps they had arrived and the marquess and Belinda had not troubled to wake her. She opened the carriage door and climbed down.

There was a farmer, leaning on a gate with a farm-hand beside him. Both were looking up at the box. The farmer had a large steel watch in one hand. 'Reckon that be about five minutes, Ham,' he said.

'Reckon as it do,' agreed Ham with a salacious leer.

Hannah joined them and looked up at the box. The marquess and Belinda were wrapped in each other's arms, both rock-still, their lips joined in a long kiss.

'Been like that this age, mum,' said the farmer cheerfully. 'Ham, here, was saying as how he'd choke were he to do that there, but I says to him that he do breathe through his mouth the whole time, which is why he couldn't achieve it. Wunnerful it is. Never seen the like.'

'My lord!' called Hannah angrily. 'You are making a spectacle of yourself.'

The marquess started, released Belinda and looked down. 'And so we are,' he said cheerfully. 'Climb in again, Miss Pym. We are on our way.'

Hannah climbed in and sat bolt upright. Their faces

had been, yes *transfigured* by love. As the carriage rolled on, a slow tear rolled down Hannah's cheek. She felt old and lonely. The feelings of precious independence given her by that legacy seemed to be withering away. No strong man had ever looked at Hannah Pym like that. No man ever would.

She had always been cheerful and hopeful. She considered life had treated her well. She had never known disease or infirmity or starvation, never regretted her spinster state. But now she felt weak and childlike and lost.

A thin ray of sunlight shone into the carriage. Hannah looked out. They were travelling quickly now along a high ridge of land. The fields stretched out, calm and peaceful, and with only a few remaining patches of snow. Her spirits began to lift. Here she was, plain Hannah Pym, off on another adventure and assisting in the marriage of a marquess. She shook her head, wondering how she could have become so blue-devilled only a moment ago.

'It must have been that venison,' said the ever-practical Hannah Pym. She rubbed her crooked nose and straightened her square shoulders.

Monks Parton was a small, sleepy village, unchanged since Tudor times. Houses of timber and wattle and thatch crouched around a triangle of village green like so many shabby cats. Two women were drawing water from a well at the edge of the village green. The marquess called down to them, asking them if they had seen any sign of a portly gentleman in clericals and an equally portly lady, driving a pony and gig.

One of the women shook her head but vouchsafed that there was a small tavern at the end of the village that had three bedchambers for guests.

The marquess drove on. The tavern, called the Bear and Stump, was as old as the houses of the village. One end of it sagged towards the ground, and the beetling thatch over the dormer windows reminded Belinda of Penelope's false eyebrows.

'I am coming with you,' said Belinda firmly, when the marquess showed signs of leaving her behind. 'She will not feel quite so humiliated if there is another woman there to comfort her.'

Hannah was determined to be 'in at the kill', but for less charitable reasons. Although she felt they were only doing their duty, she did not like either the moralizing Miss Wimple or the pontificating Mr Biles and was looking forward to seeing the guilty pair brought down a peg.

Before the marquess could stop her, Belinda had rushed before him into the inn, demanding of the landlord whether there was a Miss Wimple in residence.

The landlord, a stocky fellow in a smock who looked more like a labourer than the host of a tavern, scratched his head and said he had no one of that name.

'Then,' said the marquess, stepping in front of Belinda and Hannah, 'we are also looking for a married couple by the name of Biles.'

'Ho, them,' said the landlord. 'They's here, right enough. Room at the top o' the stairs.'

Belinda made a dart for the stairs but the marquess drew her back. 'Pray give them my card, landlord, and ask them to step below, if you would be so good.'

Belinda waited impatiently while the landlord backed towards the stairs with many low bows. 'Why do we not go up?' she asked.

'Age and passion do not mix in your young mind,' said the marquess. 'You might find yourself faced with a highly embarrassing tableau were you to burst into their room.'

There were sounds of a sharp altercation from above and then the landlord returned. 'Take a seat in the tap, my lord, my ladies, and they'll be down direct.'

'There is no back way by which they might escape?' asked the marquess.

'No, my lord. Window's too small for a gurt woman like her.'

They waited uneasily in the tap, sitting in front of a log fire.

After half an hour, Mr Biles and Miss Wimple entered. He had abandoned his clericals and was dressed in a coat with a high velvet collar and brass buttons. Miss Wimple was wearing a white-striped cotton dress printed in a tiny flowing floral pattern in red and blue and yellow. On her head, she wore a splendid cap of the same material. Both looked mulish and defiant.

Belinda rose and ran forward and took her companion's hands in her own. 'Miss Wimple,' she said, 'you have been sadly deceived. This man is married.'

'I know,' said Miss Wimple crossly, tugging her hands free.

'But *Miss Wimple*! What of all your strictures, your moralizing?'

'My love for this gentleman is pure,' said Miss Wimple, her eyes flashing. 'Hardly a love that such as you, Miss Earle, would understand.'

'Mr Biles,' said the marquess, 'what do you plan to do about your unfortunate wife?'

'Miss Wimple is now my wife, before God,' said Mr Biles, raising his hands to heaven.

'But not before man,' said the marquess drily. 'I repeat, what of your wife?'

'She may divorce me,' he said coldly. 'She has her own money. She will not starve.'

'But Miss Wimple may do so,' said the marquess, 'if your fickle fancy lights on another lady.'

'Never!' cried the pair in unison.

The marquess looked at Belinda, who gave a little despairing shrug.

'Then all I can do,' said the marquess, 'is counsel you to get as far away from the Earl of Twitterton as possible. For although you returned his carriage, in his eyes you may have stolen it, if only for a brief time, and if he presses charges against you, you will be transported.'

'You sully our great love with your warnings and fears,' said Miss Wimple grandly.

'Tcha!' snorted Hannah Pym. 'We are wasting our time here. You are a fallen woman, Miss Wimple, and I am only amazed that you can still try to hang on to the high moral ground. Come, Miss Earle.'

Belinda was glad to escape. As they stood together beside the marquess's carriage, she said in an amazed voice, 'And I thought she would be so grateful to be rescued. Where now?'

'To Lady Bellamy,' said the marquess. 'Journey's end and life's beginning.'

She's made a romantic of him, thought Hannah.

Belinda looked at Hannah shyly. 'Miss Pym, would you do me the very great honour of residing with me for a few days? I confess I dread to think of being alone with my aunt.'

'Gladly,' said Hannah. 'But you must not enter Bath on the box of his lordship's carriage. That would not do at all.'

Tired and weary, they reached Lady Bellamy's in Glossop Street. The marquess told Belinda he would call on her great-aunt that afternoon, kissed her hand, and then mounted to the box of the carriage again.

Hannah rapped on the door. An old butler opened it and informed them that Lady Bellamy was in the Green Saloon on the first floor.

Belinda clutched Hannah's arm as they mounted the stairs. 'I am feeling unaccountably nervous,' she said, glancing around. 'This place is like a prison.'

Hannah nodded in agreement. The hall had been bare except for one side-table. The staircase was uncarpeted, which was not unusual, but there were no pictures on the walls and the window on the landing above them was barred.

The butler opened the double doors, took their cards, and announced them in a surprisingly loud voice.

Belinda's heart sank right down to her little green kid slippers when she saw her great-aunt. Lady Bellamy had always been a hard-faced, austere woman, but she looked even more grim and disapproving than Belinda remembered her to be. The first thing Hannah noticed was not her ladyship, but the fact that the windows of the Green Saloon were barred as well.

She then turned her attention to Lady Bellamy. She was a tall, gaunt woman dressed in a gown that looked like sackcloth. A Bible lay on a small table beside her. She put out a hand and rested it on the cover of the Bible and Hannah noticed that hand was so thin, it was almost transparent. Her eyes were black and glittering, as if she had a fever.

'So the fallen one has come,' said Lady Bellamy in a deep voice that had a hollow ring to it, as if sounded from the depths of a tomb.

'Miss Earle is here, yes,' said Hannah.

'And who are you?'

'I am Miss Hannah Pym of Kensington,' said Hannah, meeting that black, glittering gaze with a steady one of her own. 'Unfortunately, Miss Earle's companion has fallen from grace. She is run off with a Methodist preacher. Miss Earle has requested that I stay with her for a few days.'

'That you may not.' Lady Bellamy's glance dismissed Hannah and fastened on Belinda. 'I shall soon teach you the error of your ways, young miss. Running off with a footman, indeed! Too much food. Nothing like starvation to purge the soul.'

Belinda flashed a scared look at Hannah, and then said, 'My lady, I have good news. Lord Frenton, the Marquess of Frenton, has done me the honour to offer me his hand in marriage and I have accepted. He is to call upon you this afternoon to ask leave to pay his addresses.'

'Frenton? Frenton of Baddell Castle?'

'The same.'

'You poor child. Do not worry. I shall keep you pure.'

'Mad,' Hannah mouthed to Belinda.

Aloud, she said to Lady Bellamy, 'Your great-niece has secured a fine match for herself. Surely congratulations are the order of the day.'

'Never!' cried Lady Bellamy. 'What is this year?'

'Eighteen hundred,' said Hannah impatiently, wondering how soon she could get Belinda away from this madwoman.

'Then let me see ... it was in ninety-two that Frenton caused such a scandal in our fair city. Lady Devine had been widowed but two years when he dragged her into his bed. They lived together quite openly.'

Belinda turned pale. 'And where is Lady Devine now?'

'She married the Duke of Minster. The wicked flourish like the green bay tree.' She looked at Hannah. 'Miss What's-your-name, take yourself off.'

162

'I shall just see Miss Pym to the door,' said Belinda, clutching Hannah even harder.

Lady Bellamy jerked the bell-rope twice. The aged butler and two young footmen appeared. 'Bradfield,' said Lady Bellamy to the butler, 'show this lady out. You two, James and Henry, take Miss Earle to her bedchamber and lock her in. You know I have everything prepared for her arrival.'

Hannah was carrying her trusty umbrella. It was a heavy thing, covered in green waxcloth and with iron spokes. She raised it menacingly and stood in front of Belinda. 'Stand aside,' she shouted. 'I am taking Miss Earle with me.'

Lady Bellamy seemed indifferent. 'Lock them in together,' she commanded.

The two footmen approached. Belinda darted for the door, wrenched her bad ankle and collapsed to the ground with a cry of pain. Hannah dropped her umbrella and ran to her.

She helped Belinda to her feet. She could not start a fight and risk injuring Belinda further. As long as she was to be locked in with Belinda, they might plan something between them.

Urged forward by the footmen, Hannah, her arm around Belinda's waist, helped her up the stairs. They were thrust into a room and the door was locked behind them.

Both stood still, looking helplessly around. 'Mad,' said Belinda, beginning to cry. 'She's gone raving mad.'

Hannah nodded gloomily. There was an old double

bed without curtains or posts, covered in a ragged quilt. Apart from that, there was no other furniture except a prie-dieu in the corner. The windows were barred.

'Now what are we going to do?' said Hannah Pym.

8

Adventure is to the adventurous.

Benjamin Disraeli

The marquess, reluctant all at once to see his sister and to have to explain his sudden engagement and endure all the questions he knew she would throw at him, put up at the Pelican Inn.

He bathed and washed the powder out of his hair and dressed with great care. He felt a lightness of spirit, an absence of loneliness. Soon he would see Belinda again.

He made his way on foot to Glossop Street. An elderly butler answered the door and said courteously that the ladies were not at home, they were out walking.

The marquess was angry. He had said he would call. 'I am staying at the Pelican,' he said stiffly, handing over his card. 'Be so good as to tell the ladies to send for me when they find themselves available to receive me.'

He walked away huffily, his spirits low. What could have happened?

He returned in the evening and looked bewildered when he was met with the same reply. He noticed the old butler could not meet his eyes. So they were lying. Belinda had changed her mind. A pox on all women.

He returned to the Pelican and ordered a bottle of wine and sat moodily in the tap. And then he saw Colonel Harry Audley bearing down on him. He knew the colonel of old and damned him as the biggest bore in Bath.

'Just come to the city, Frenton?' asked the colonel, sitting down beside him without asking permission.

'Yes, and enjoying my own company,' said the marquess pointedly.

The colonel ignored him and began to prose on about who was in society in Bath and what they had said to him and what he had said to them. The marquess half-closed his eyes and drank his wine and waited for the colonel to dry up and go away.

Dimly, the colonel's voice penetrated his worried brain. '. . . and quite mad, if you ask me. When old Bellamy died she came to The Bath and we were all prepared to be kind to her, but she got seized with a sort of religious mania. Then she began to see thieves and burglars everywhere. That house of hers in Glossop Street is like a prison.'

'Whose house?' asked the marquess suddenly.

'Ain't I been telling you, dear boy? Lady Bellamy.'

'Tell me again.'

The colonel looked gratified at having secured an interested audience at last. 'Mad as Dick's hatband is Lady Bellamy. You should take a walk down Glossop Street and have a look at her house. Bars on every window. She occasionally walks out and has two strong footmen to guard her, just as if she expected one of the invalids of The Bath to savage her. Why, I call to mind—'

'Good evening,' said the marquess, got to his feet, and hurried out.

Sharp anxiety stabbed at his heart. He now did not believe for a moment that Belinda was avoiding him.

Hannah and Belinda sat miserably in the cold, dark room that was their prison.

'She hasn't come yet,' said Hannah. 'I am so hungry and thirsty. Wait until I see that aunt and uncle of yours. When I reach London, *if* I ever reach London, I am going straight to them and I am going to give them a piece of my mind. How dare they send you here? That woman is mad. It must be well known in Bath. When did you last see her?'

'Seven years ago,' said Belinda. 'She was all right in her head then, but very moralizing. The whole of Sunday was taken up with readings from the Bible and sermons.'

'And what can Frenton be thinking of?' demanded Hannah. 'He will have called. He cannot believe we would not see him.'

Belinda turned her head away. 'He may prefer the charms of Lady Devine.'

'Now, don't start that!' cried Hannah. 'Ain't we miserable enough? Mark my words, he pleasured himself with a willing widow who can't have had her reputation damned by the liaison because she's now a duchess. Get some sense in your head and refute everything that madwoman has told you.'

A voice sounded behind the door. It was Lady Bellamy. 'I hope you are praying for the salvation of your souls,' she said sonorously. 'You will be allowed a morsel of bread and water, which will be brought to you in five minutes. My footman will be armed, so do not make any trouble. Tomorrow, I shall come and read to you.'

Belinda and Hannah looked at each other in the gloom.

'At least we'll get a drink of water,' said Belinda.

Hannah's eyes fell on her trusty umbrellas, propped in a corner. She lowered her voice to a whisper. 'When this footman comes, I will stand behind the door and hit him on the head with my umbrella. It should be easy to stun him. The umbrella has a silver knob.'

'What if you hit too hard and kill him?' asked Belinda with a shiver. 'Or what if you do not hit hard enough and he shoots *me*?'

'Quite simple,' said the ever-practical Hannah Pym. 'You dart to one side just as I strike him.'

Belinda began to tremble. 'I am afraid of guns,' she said.

'Courage. We must have courage,' said Hannah firmly, 'else we shall be kept here and go as mad as that lunatic great-aunt of yours.'

Belinda wrinkled her brow in thought. Then she said slowly, 'Great-Aunt Harriet is mad, but the footman is not. They are just two strong young men who are being well paid to perform their duties. The footman who is bringing us the bread and water may be armed, but he will not shoot us. He would not dare.'

'True,' said Hannah. 'But I do not think we can risk it. He may just fire without thinking.'

The Marquess of Frenton knocked at Lady Bellamy's door again. Again the butler opened it, but this time the marquess lifted him up by the elbows and set him aside, then walked past him. 'Help!' shouted the butler.

The marquess bounded up the stairs.

At the same time, the footman unlocked the door of Belinda and Hannah's room and entered, carrying a tray in one hand and a gun in the other.

The room was in darkness and he could only make out the blurred whiteness of a face in the far corner.

'Now!' cried Hannah Pym, bringing her umbrella down on his head with all her might. Belinda dived under the bed. There was an almighty crash as the tray and the gun went flying and the footman measured his length on the floor.

The marquess heard that crash but found his way barred by the other footman. He only paused for a moment and then ran up as the footman spread out his arms to bar the way. For a split second, the marquess thought ruefully of his knuckles, already bruised from having punched Lord Frederick, and then he drove his fist full in the footman's stomach. The footman doubled up. The marquess swerved past him and went up to where the sound of the crash had come from.

His heart was beating hard against his ribs as he saw a dark figure stretched on the floor. Hannah saw his silhouette in the gloom and raised her umbrella again.

'Belinda!' called the marquess. The umbrella dropped from Hannah's suddenly nerveless fingers. 'Here, my lord,' she called.

'Where is Belinda?'

'Under the bed.'

'Who is that on the floor?'

'A footman. I hit him.'

'Light. We must have light.' The marquess went into the passage. An oil-lamp was burning in a niche at the far end. He brought it into the room and held it high. Belinda crawled out from under the bed. 'Get us out of here, Richard,' she begged. 'Great-Aunt Harriet is run mad.'

The footman on the floor groaned and stirred. 'Thank God,' whispered Hannah. 'I have not killed him.'

'Follow me,' ordered the marquess. He caught Belinda around the waist as she hobbled up to him and kissed her quickly on the mouth.

They followed him down the shadowy stairs past the footman the marquess had struck. He was sitting on the stairs holding his stomach. As they went down to the hall, Hannah said, 'Wait! I am going to give that Lady Bellamy a piece of my mind.'

'No!' said the marquess. 'That can come later. Outside.'

'I command you to stay,' called a voice from the stairs.

They turned and looked up.

Lady Bellamy was standing on the upper landing, holding a candle under her chin so that her white face and glittering black eyes appeared to be suspended in the blackness.

The marquess threw her one horrified look and shoved both Hannah and Belinda outside into the street.

'We will go to the Pelican,' he said. 'Then we will decide what to do.' He put his arm around Belinda again and helped her along and she leaned against him and felt she had been transported from hell to heaven.

They all had an enormous supper at the Pelican and then the marquess excused himself, saying there were things he had to do.

Belinda and Hannah, who were sharing a room, waited for his return anxiously.

He came back about midnight, with two of the inn servants carrying Belinda's and Hannah's luggage.

'How did you get it?' asked Belinda, wide-eyed.

'I returned with two of the parish constables and the watch. Lady Bellamy was all help and charm. She showed them a letter from your parents, Belinda, in which they had urged her to chastise you as she saw fit. Locking young relatives up in rooms with only bread and water is an everyday happening. She showered the constables and the watchman with gold and apologized for having caused them to be brought out so late at night. I asked for your luggage and she ordered a footman, one with a bandaged head, Miss Pym, to bring the trunks.'

'When we left, one of the constables, who was an old man, talked to me like a father and said it was wrong of me to drink so deep and frighten the poor old lady.'

Belinda and Hannah exclaimed at this and Hannah was all for going back and tackling the authorities, but the marquess said he had Belinda safe and was not going to let her go again. He did not want to see any other relatives.

'You'll have to see 'em,' said Hannah. 'You'll have to take Miss Earle back to London and ask her aunt and uncle.'

'I have decided I am not going to see them,' said the marquess. 'If Belinda is returned to London, I am forced into a long courtship!' He turned to Belinda. 'I have my travelling carriage. What say you to a Gretna marriage? We can return as man and wife and be married properly in church at our leisure.'

Belinda clasped her hands. 'I would like that of all things.'

'But if her aunt and uncle do not approve of the marriage, Miss Earle will not gain her inheritance,' protested Hannah.

'A fig on her inheritance,' said the marquess. 'You may come to Gretna with us if you wish, Miss Pym.'

But Hannah thought of being alongside such an amorous pair and shook her head. 'I will take the stage back to London. But I will see your aunt and uncle, Miss Earle, and give them a piece of my mind.'

Hannah went out to the inn courtyard the following morning to say goodbye to the happy couple. Belinda was sitting on the box beside the marquess. Hannah opened her mouth to protest and then reflected that they were to be married, albeit unconventionally, and so appearances did not matter any more.

Belinda sat silently beside the marquess until the city of Bath was left far behind. Then he slowed his horses and smiled down at her. 'I wonder if I shall ever forget Miss Pym,' said Belinda.

'No need to forget her,' said the marquess. 'I have her address. She may dance at our wedding – that is, when we are properly married.'

'You are so good, Richard,' sighed Belinda. She had decided not to mention the famous or infamous Lady Devine. Hannah had told her last night that was all in the past and gentlemen did not like to be reminded of old amours.

'Good, am I?' The marquess stopped the carriage and took her in his arms. He fell to kissing her passionately until his much-goaded tiger bawled out, 'Get a move on, me lord, or we'll never get to heathen parts' – heathen parts being Scotland.

* * *

173

Hannah, too, considered the marquess a very good man. She returned to the room she had shared with Belinda to find he had left a letter of thanks and a purse of gold for her. She walked back out into the sunny morning, and bought a very dashing bonnet in Milsom Street, plus a cashmere shawl and a new umbrella, a replica of the one she had broken hitting the footman. She booked a ticket on the stage-coach that was to leave the following day. On her return to the Pelican, she sat down at a desk in the coffee room and wrote a brief letter to Sir George Clarence, telling him of the day of her return, and reminding him of his promise to show her the gardens. Hannah wanted his reply to be there, waiting for her, when she got home.

She felt very rich now that the marquess's gold was added to her legacy. She would perhaps ask Sir George to put it in the bank for her. But then she changed her mind. She would use up the gold first on her travels and save her legacy. Besides, it gave her a feeling of comfort to think of all those gleaming sovereigns reposing at the bottom of her large reticule.

She tried on her new hat, called a Grecian bonnet. Hannah thought it so becoming that she took herself to the Pump Room for tea and enjoyed herself immensely.

As she climbed aboard the stage-coach next day to set out for London, she scanned the faces of the other passengers eagerly, but decided that her adventures were over for the present. There were an enormously fat lady with a thin little husband, a doctor and a sailor, and four noisy bloods on the roof, who promised embarrassment rather than adventure on the road home. Fortunately for Hannah, the bloods drank themselves into a state of oblivion before Devizes was reached and the whole journey to London passed without incident.

She found herself quite breathless with excitement as she climbed the stairs to her flat above the bakery in the village of Kensington. But when she unlocked the door and went inside, there was no letter there. She descended to the bakery to learn with a sinking heart that there had been no post for her at all.

Hannah waited a whole week. At last she felt so low in spirits that she called on Belinda's aunt and uncle and gave them a piece of her mind.

'I do not understand,' wailed Mrs Earle after her maid had brought her out of the swoon Hannah's news had caused. 'A marquess! Why should she run away?'

Hannah told them roundly of all Belinda's adventures, ending up with her treatment at the hands of her great-aunt. 'So I suggest,' ended Hannah, 'that you write to Baddell Castle and tell the new Marchioness of Frenton how very sorry you are!'

Feeling slightly more cheerful, and more hopeful, Hannah returned to her flat. Surely that precious letter would be there by now. But it did not arrive. She felt the time had come to set out on her travels again. But surely Sir George would write. Another long week passed, a week during which Hannah Pym began to feel like a presumptuous servant who did not know her place, expecting someone as grand and handsome as Sir George Clarence to pay her any attention whatsoever.

The Marquess of Frenton propped himself up on one elbow and looked down at his wife, who was lying in the bed beside him.

She was awake and looking up at the bed canopy with a vague stare.

'Thinking of me?' he said in a teasing voice.

'No,' replied Belinda, 'I was thinking of Miss Pym.'

'Darling and dearest, we have just travelled to heaven and back this night and all you can think about is Hannah Pym!'

Belinda stretched her naked body and smiled up at him.

'I was thinking how nice it would be if Miss Pym married Sir George Clarence.'

'Clarence? Old stick who used to be in the diplomatic corps?'

'Possibly. It is all very romantic, you see.' Belinda told her husband of Hannah's rise up through the servants' ranks and then of that legacy. 'And Sir George took her to tea at Gunter's, and he has promised to show her the gardens at Thornton Hall on her return.'

'Romance and Miss Pym do not mix. She is always practical. She thought we would suit very well and she was right, for there is more to marriage than bed, and you enchant me even when you are fully dressed.'

'Did Lady Devine enchant you?' asked Belinda, forgetting Hannah's good advice.

'She amused me and I her for a little while. That is all.'

'Are you sure that is all?' asked Belinda.

'Have I not just said so?' he demanded angrily. 'I believed that fairy tale of yours as related by Miss Pym about the footman, and that was hard to swallow, believe me!'

'It was all true,' said Belinda wrathfully. 'You are a pig and a beast. You didn't believe me at all. You only pretended to.'

'I am going to get dressed,' he said in a flat voice. He swung his legs out of bed. Belinda surveyed his naked back in dismay. Tears started to her eyes. Their marriage was over before it had begun. She gave a choked sob.

He immediately turned around and then got back into bed and gathered her into her arms. 'I am a brute, Belinda,' he said softly. He caressed her naked breast and smiled down into her tear-filled eyes.

'Do not let us quarrel ever again, Richard,' said Belinda.

'Not ever,' he promised fervently.

But of course they did, violently and bitterly, from time to time, and so had a normal and happy marriage.

Hannah roused herself from her despair. Cold frosty nights and sunny days made fine weather for travelling, and the roads of England stretched out from London, holding excitement and adventure.

But before she left again, she would walk out of the

village and along the Kensington road and look in at the grounds of Thornton Hall. Looking at the grounds and the improvements would give her something to take with her on her next journey. She would not go in through the gates but just stand and look.

She walked along in the sunlight, feeling better than she had since she left Bath. She was approaching the place where she had worked all those long years, the place *he* now owned.

Soon she saw the familiar roofs of Thornton Hall rising above the bare branches of the trees. Trees! Hannah stopped and stared. For there had been no trees at Thornton Hall, only acres of grass kept down by a flock of sheep. Mrs Clarence had wanted a garden and had started a rose garden at the back of the house. After she had fled, Hannah had done her best to keep it in order, just in case Mrs Clarence came back, but Mrs Clarence had not come back, and gradually the weeds had encroached on the rose garden.

She walked more quickly now, until she was standing before the familiar iron gates. She looked through them in awe. An avenue of lime-trees marched all the way up to the house. There seemed to be men working everywhere – men digging over the ground, men planting – and there, supervising the work, stood the tall figure of Sir George Clarence.

All Hannah's newfound lightness of spirits fled. He had not troubled to reply to her letter. She turned sadly away.

Something made Sir George look down the long

avenue. He saw the figure of a lady at the gates, and as she turned to leave, he thought he recognized those hunting shoulders, square and sharp-edged. He gave an exclamation and said to one of the gardeners, 'Run to the gates. There is a lady wearing a Grecian bonnet who has just left. Catch up with her, and if she be a Miss Pym, bring her back with you.'

Hannah trudged along. She did not want to go travelling again. How she had dreamt of telling him of her latest adventures. Now she had no one to tell. She felt old and alone and friendless.

'Miss Pym!'

Hannah swung around.

A gardener came running up to her. Her gave a jerky bow and asked, 'Be you Miss Pym?'

'I am she,' said Hannah.

'Sir George wishes to speak to you, mum.'

'Very well,' said Hannah, not knowing that at that moment her face had become as transfigured by love as Belinda's had been when the marquess told her he loved her.

By the time she returned to the gates with the gardener, Sir George was waiting for her, his bright-blue eyes studying her curiously. 'What is the meaning of this, Miss Pym?' he cried. 'I am anxious to show you the gardens. Why did you not enter?'

'I did not think I would be welcome,' said Hannah, suddenly as shy as a young girl. 'I wrote to you, sir, but you never replied to my letter.'

'But I am just returned from the north. I have been visiting an old friend. You are not the only traveller,

Miss Pym. I came straight here. But now you are here, let me show you what we are planning.'

'How did you get those trees to grow so quickly?' asked Hannah, while she took rapid mental inventory of her appearance. Grecian bonnet bought in Bath, latest fashion, very good. Dark-brown printed linen 'two-piece', not Mrs Clarence's, but bought from a dressmaker in Green Street, who had made it up for a lady who had gone abroad and showed no signs of returning, so Hannah had been able to purchase it for very little. Fashionable. The brown linen was patterned with tiny leaves of red, white and greeny-brown. It had a high-waisted jacket with a matching frill and long sleeves ending in a frill almost covering each green-gloved hand. Her shoes were of green calfskin with a small heel, and she wore stockings in the new shade of olive green. She longed for the courage to loop her gown over one arm to display a leg, as the young ladies did, for Hannah was proud of her legs, but guessed rightly it would be considered unbecoming in one of her years.

'I had them put in fully grown, a whole avenue of lime-trees,' said Sir George. 'And come over here, Miss Pym. We are digging an ornamental lake.'

'So you plan to keep Thornton Hall?'

'I do not think so,' said Sir George. 'Gardening is my passion, and when the gardens are finished, they will add considerably to the value of the house.'

He led her through the gardens in the sunshine, describing plants and bushes, and Hannah listened in a happy daze, barely hearing what he said, aware that he was talking to her as he would talk to an equal. She was enjoying looking at his high-nosed face, his silvery-white hair, and his eyes, which were as blue as the cloudless sky above. There was a smell of warm, newly turned earth. A thrush sang on a swaying branch and Hannah turned her head quickly away to hide the fact that her eyes were full of happy tears.

'So, now,' he said finally, 'we must have tea and hear your adventures. The caretaker's wife is poorly at the moment, but I have my carriage and there is always Gunter's, is there not, Miss Pym?'

Oh, thank heaven for Gunter's, thought Hannah, sitting beside Sir George in an open carriage as they bowled through Hyde Park toll. Gunter's, the confectioners in Berkeley Square, was one of the most fashionable rendezvous in London.

'Now,' said Sir George when they were facing each other over a lavish spread of tea and cakes, 'tell me your news.'

Hannah's odd eyes flashed green. 'Once upon a time,' she began, and Sir George settled back to listen to her tale with every appearance of a man prepared to enjoy himself.

And what a tale it was, reflected Sir George in amazement. There were the singing Judds; the carriage in the river; the beautiful Belinda, for Hannah did now remember Belinda as beautiful; the handsome marquess; and the wicked Penelope. He sat there, his tea forgotten, the cakes uneaten, as the story unwound, ending with the terrible Lady Bellamy and the flight to Gretna.

'Well, by Jove,' he exclaimed when she had finished. 'I really think you should stay in London, Miss Pym. You attract adventures like a magnet. You are a brave and resourceful matchmaker if ever there was one. Surely you have had your fill of adventures now?'

Hannah shook her head. The wicked thought flashed through her mind that she would stay in London for the rest of her life, if only she could sit with him like this for half an hour a day. But she dreaded boring him, dreaded the day when he might consider he was becoming too friendly with this ex-servant of his brother. As yet, Hannah believed she was not in love with Sir George. She admired him greatly, she basked in the warmth of his interest, but that was all.

'So where shall you go next?'

Hannah looked bewildered. 'I have not thought about it,' she said, remembering those long days filled with misery waiting for that letter that never came.

'The Portsmouth road is a good one,' said Sir George, calling for the waiter to take away the pot of tea, which had grown cold while he listened to Hannah's adventures, and bring a fresh pot.

'Portsmouth!' Golden eyes looked at him. I have it, he thought, amused. Miss Pym's eyes are blue when she is sad, green when she is excited, and golden when she is happy.

'That is at the sea, is it not?' asked Hannah.

'Of course it is. A famous port which has seen many kings and queens. Robert, Duke of Normandy, landed there in 1101, bent on an argument with his brother Henry as to who should wear the crown. Richard the First gave the town its first charter. And at Portsmouth in the thirteenth century, I think, the first oranges were landed in England from a Spanish vessel as a present for the Castilian wife of Edward the First.'

'I have never seen the sea,' said Hannah.

'Then I hope you arrive in fine weather and not in a fog.'

'And what will you be doing, sir?' asked Hannah.

'I shall lead my usual idle life, going to my club, working on the gardens, travelling to see old friends.'

Hannah wondered if any of the old friends were ladies but did not have the courage to find out.

He began to talk of his travels while he had been in the diplomatic corps. But although he had travelled widely in foreign countries, he did not seem to have had any wild adventures such as Hannah Pym had experienced travelling on the English stage-coach. Hannah listened to his voice. She wished she could take home something from Gunter's to remind her of this day. Chip a piece off the table, take a saucer – something, anything, to tell herself in later years that she had not dreamt it all. Then she noticed that the waiter had put an extra teaspoon beside her saucer by mistake. It was a small silver spoon stamped 'Gunter's'.

Hannah covered it with her handkerchief, and when Sir George lifted the lid of the teapot to see if there was any tea left, she slipped that spoon into her reticule.

They talked for another hour, and then Sir George remembered he had been invited to dinner and must go home and change.

He offered to drive her to Kensington, but Hannah said she would walk to the White Bear in Piccadilly and purchase a ticket for the Portsmouth coach.

He walked her to the corner of the square, swept off his hat, and kissed her gloved hand. And then he said the words that Hannah had prayed he might say.

'Do not forget to let me know when you next return, Miss Pym. I shall not be going out of London for the next few weeks, so I shall be here to receive any letter you may send. Do take care and do not become involved in any more dangerous adventures.'

'I am sure I shall have a very quiet journey,' said Hannah. 'I did not tell you, but the return journey from Bath was boring.'

He laughed and said, 'You will soon be content to stay in London once the Season begins.'

'I am afraid the London Season will not affect me, nor I it,' said Hannah.

He looked at her in surprise, as if remembering for the first time that day that this lady was his brother's former housekeeper. 'But you must sample some of the delights of the Season, Miss Pym. Tell you what – you let me know when you are coming back and I will take you to the opera.'

Hannah curtsied low. 'Thank you, sir,' she said. 'I shall look forward to it.'

He watched her as she walked off. He felt she should not be walking about London unescorted.

Then he remembered his appointment and hurried off.

Hannah walked towards Piccadilly, breathing rapidly.

'Oh, my heart,' she muttered. 'My poor heart will burst with gladness.'

But she remembered her duty and suddenly swung about and marched back to Gunter's, and told little Mr Gunter firmly that she had taken one of his teaspoons with her as a memento and would now like to pay for it. She had not liked to do so in front of the gentleman.

Mr Gunter was not surprised, thinking that Hannah must be of the Quality, and he was used to humouring their little eccentricities.

So Hannah Pym slept that night in her narrow bed with the spoon under her pillow along with the glove he had kissed.